LOCK 'EM DOWN

A TENNESSEE THUNDERBOLTS NOVEL

BANG BROTHERS HOCKEY
BOOK 4

GINA AZZI

THREE CITIES PUBLISHING LLC

LOCK 'EM DOWN

Print ISBN-13: 978-1-954470-79-8
Ebook ISBN-13: 978-1-954470-47-7

BANG BROTHERS HOCKEY SERIES

Meet the Bang Brothers—five hot hockey-playing brothers who are allergic to commitment.
The brothers are about to face off against their newly-retired mother...who suddenly has plenty of time to play matchmaker. Add in their baby sister and some secret dating, a single dad, an accidental pregnancy, a marriage of convenience, and a wrong bed—or two—and these siblings are not going to know what hit them!

Lace 'em Up
Show 'em How
Hit 'em Hard
Lock 'em Down
Light 'em Up
Hook 'em Hard

FROM THE JOURNAL OF STELLA BANG

Dear Diane,

It's hard to believe you're gone. More than hard; it's devastating. Lars says time will ease the band of pressure that cuts across my chest when I think of you. But no amount of time will make me miss you any less. I suppose the passing years will only result in an acceptance of reality.

I lost my best friend.

Just the other day, I picked up the phone to tell you about the twins' mess at school. It involved crazy glue (stolen from the teacher's supply closet) and googly eyes! Needless to say, Jakob was NOT happy. He's been so serious and severe the last few years; it's a good thing he has the twins to make him crack a smile now and then.

Anyway, I picked up the phone to tell you, and then I remembered. Oh, the waves of anguish are unbearable and relentless whenever I remember. My therapist says that's normal. In fact, it was her idea that I write to you. She said it could be cathartic. Healing.

Little does she know we'd uncork a bottle of wine and spill our guts, no doubt dissolving in laughter, whenever one of us needed to heal a heartache. Your bad breakup with Joe. My sadness when Jakob divorced. Your mother's passing. Leif nearly being expelled from university. We've seen each other through all the ups and downs.

It's difficult for me to move forward and start a new chapter without you.

But I bought this diary. And now, I'm sitting here, at the kitchen table, writing to you.

The house is quiet. Lars left early for practice. And the kids... They're all grown up. After years of pinching their cheeks and reminding them that mother knows best, they're out into the world. Blazing trails and finding their footing.

That's another reason I can't accept you're gone. You, Diane, with your flashing blue eyes, loud, boisterous laughter, and penchant for mischief—how can you be gone? I contacted your niece and nephews after your funeral. They were kind and gracious. But they don't remember you the way I do. I'm not sure anyone does. And that sits heavy on my chest, keeping me up at night.

What's a life without love? Without friendship? Without family?

Lars and I are coming up on thirty-five years of marriage. I know how fortunate I am to have married the love of my life and then stayed married for thirty-five wonderful years. I'm blessed to have birthed six healthy, beautiful children who all pursued their passions and are making their way in the world.

And yet, I can't help but wonder—are they fulfilled? None of them are close to family. None of them have found or kept love. They're...adrift. Just like you were before I forced you to join my family. "An honorary Bang," you laughed. But I saw the happiness it brought you. It was the same happiness I felt.

King's in his thirties and hasn't had a serious relationship since college. Jakob is a single parent struggling with raising children on his own. Jensen and Annie are still thick as thieves but on opposite ends of the country. Leif avoids commitment like the plague. And Tanner's living his best life, partying like it's his job.

When will they settle down? Find the type of happiness I've known for over half my life? I don't mean to sound old-fashioned—although I can admit that I am in many ways, but I want more grandbabies. And to know that my children are fulfilled. Happy. In love.

I want them to find what Lars and I share. Love, respect, commitment. Trust.

I want them to have everything I wished for you, Diane. And perhaps the most challenging part of letting you go is knowing you didn't have the great big love you desired.

It's true what they say: life is too short.

Which is why I have an idea. A plan, really, although I haven't told Lars yet. I think the kids—all of them— need help. A mother's touch, so to speak, since I obviously know best. And, with Lars coaching the junior league, he's either at the rink or traveling with the team. Most of the time, I'm on my own. It's lonely without you to come by for a cup of tea or meet for lunch. Depressingly so.

My therapist thinks a change of scenery will help. She thinks I should shake up my routine.

And so... What if I visit them? The kids. I can help

them. *Cook their favorite meals. Look after the boys so Jakob can go on a date or two. Give them the nudges they need or, in some cases, the well-placed shoves. It will be an adventure, Diane! For all of us.*

I just need to run it by Lars, but...soon, I'll write to you from King's place in Oakland. Isn't that grand? I'll be living my best life in the sunshine well before the first snowstorm hits Minnesota. If you were here, I know that would delight you!

I miss you, my friend. I'll write more soon.

Love, Stella

This letter starts Stella's journey to visit her children across the US and Canada. If you haven't read the previous Bang Brothers Hockey books, the storylines spill into each other. However, you can also enjoy Leif and Cami's story as a stand-alone. Lock 'em Down is book four in the Bang Brothers Hockey series. It also takes place in the Tennessee Thunderbolts world and is book 7 in that series. Happy reading!

ONE

Cami

"You didn't tell your mom we're in Vegas?" Izzy's eyes nearly fall out of her head. She groans and places her hand over her mouth. "Cami! She's going to kill us."

"Me. Not you," I remind her cheerfully. For sure, Mom is going to be upset that I joined this last-minute graduation celebration in Vegas.

I can already hear her disapproval. *You girls went to Vegas with no parents? With no chaperones? Where anything could have happened to you?* But... "I'm moving to Tennessee. I don't know the next time I'm going to see you girls. I was *not* missing this." And I didn't have time to put in the effort I'd need to get Mom on board for this party weekend.

Izzy sighs but she glances at our group of girlfriends. Then, she looks at me, tears shimmering in her brown eyes. "I'm gonna miss you, Cam."

"Oh, jeez," I laugh, even though emotion tightens my throat. Izzy and I have been through a lot together. She showed up for me big time when I came home after a semester study in Europe, brokenhearted and broken-spirited. Then again, when Mom intervened by showing up at our college dorm nearly every Friday night, a bag of popcorn in hand and a movie recommendation in mind.

Mom's meddling became so aggressive that after she tried to set me up with her dentist's son—*a good boy, from a good family*—Izzy covered for me by corroborating my lie of having a stomach bug.

It's going to be strange not having her close by. "Come here." I toss an arm around her shoulders. "You'll come visit me in Knoxville, right?"

Izzy nods. "I can't believe you're moving next week."

I bite the corner of my mouth. I can't believe it either. While most of my college friends—fellow members of our sorority Alpha Phi—are staying in Minnesota or at least in the Midwest, I'm heading east. But the job offer—a boring position at an accounting firm with a solid starting salary—is exactly what Mom and Dad want for me.

Besides, I can use the distance from home. I need a break from my mom's incessant worrying that I'm going to throw my life away—or worse, end up with the wrong man for a husband.

As kid number three, I'm her wild card. My siblings, Rhett and Jenna, didn't pull the shenanigans I did and as such, she doubled down on me. On ensuring I didn't step too far out of line. And ever since I did, while studying abroad in Spain three years ago, she's been determined to reset my course.

Nothing would make Mom happier than me settled down, with a stable career, and a strong husband to protect and provide for me.

A weekend in Vegas? Not so much.

My mother is a helicopter parent and while I can, to a degree, appreciate her looking out for me, she constantly crosses the line.

Now, I want the chance to enjoy myself in a fun, eclectic new city. I need the freedom to make my own choices and mistakes—and maybe if I had more of it, my poor judgement calls wouldn't be such colossal blunders.

It's time for a new chapter for the new graduate.

"Girls!" Mia shouts over her shoulder, pointing at the approaching server who is balancing a tray of shot glasses. "We're doing shots."

Izzy grins. "You ready for tonight?"

"Totally," I say, meaning it. While Mom accuses me of being impulsive, I prefer to think of my spontaneity as an asset. It means I dive into things headfirst, savoring the experience and relishing the moment.

It may not have always served me well in the past, but tonight is different. With the excitement of my new life in Knoxville beckoning, I'm different. It feels like I'm on the precipice of adulthood, and for the first time in years, I trust myself to be here.

Linking my arm with Izzy's, we rejoin our friends around the table on the rooftop patio. It's filled with people of all ages and backgrounds—but everyone is in a celebratory mood. Isn't that why you come to Vegas?

To party? Let loose? Have some damn fun?

I lift my shot glass to the group. "To us!"

"Happy graduation!" Izzy exclaims, clinking her glass against mine.

"Cheers!" Mia adds.

"To tonight!" Tamara exclaims.

We take our shooters and I smack my lips together as the vodka burns a trail of heat down my throat.

"Ooh, six o'clock," Tamara murmurs.

Turning to look over my shoulder, I catch the group of attractive, well-dressed men as they saunter onto the patio.

"They look like athletes," Izzy decides.

"They look like a good fucking time," Mia laughs.

I purse my lips as I study the one who caught my eye. He's tall and built in a way that speaks to hours in the gym. A broad chest that stretches the material of his navy shirt. Shoulders that a girl can hang on to. Forearms corded with muscle.

Jesus, how can a guy's arms be so...hot?

I tilt my head, studying him. I hate that my first reaction is to compare him to Levi. In the three years since the famous musician and rhythm guitarist for the internationally acclaimed band The Burnt Clovers broke my heart, my gut instinct—my knee-jerk reaction—is always to compare a man to him.

To his wild eyes, his sexy smirk, and the way his hair stuck up in all directions. To the way he saw life as one big joke and only focused on the moment at hand.

In hindsight, Levi was a mess. Spiraling and falling apart. As evidenced by his stint in rehab after a night gone sideways. A night I'd rather forget. But in a matter of weeks, I fell in love with Levi Rousell. It was short-lived and lightning fast. A fling that soared high and burned out in an instant.

But he's still my baseline. My only true experience with intense, overwhelming emotions. The only man who's twisted me up inside. The only one I've never gotten closure from.

Of course, I've gone on dates since. I've flirted and kissed and even slept with a few. But Levi—and our time together—has followed me around like a shadow. A persistent reminder of what could be and a warning of how it can go wrong.

For the first time ever, I think this man, this stranger, could overtake Levi's impression on me. He's got that energy —a vibe—that could outshine a shadow. The thought makes me smile.

It's ridiculous and yet, my body hums with awareness.

I may be going to Knoxville as a single, independent woman, ready to begin adulthood on my own terms. But what's one last hurrah? One fun night in Vegas? One final chance to throw caution to the wind?

Mia giggles, interrupting my thoughts, and I turn to look at her.

She flips her chin at me knowingly. "You caught his attention, Cami."

Huh? I swing my eyes back to the hottie at six o'clock and my gaze slams into his.

I suck in a deep breath. Holy hell. Forget his arms. His eyes are—mesmerizing. Yeah, that's the word for them. A deep, electric blue that shocks my system by its intensity.

He holds my gaze and after a beat, the slowest, most knowing, cocky-as-hell smile curls his lips.

"Damn," Izzy mutters.

"I'll drink to that," Tamara agrees, downing another shot.

I bite my bottom lip and smirk back. I've never been coy or shy. I'm a what-you-see-is-what-you-get kind of girl and this man just looked at me in a way that I could latch onto and run with.

I mean, I'm here, aren't I? Adulthood in Knoxville is only days away and I've been biding my time in Minnesota, waiting for the opportunity to step into my own skin again. To stop being fearful or ashamed. To start living my life.

A thrill shimmies up my spine and I shake my head. Then, I take another shot of vodka to steady my nerves and clear my mind.

When I look back up, the man and his friends have taken over a corner table. They're joking with the server. Their group has a relaxed energy, as though they're just out to enjoy the night and whatever it brings.

Some tables of men hold an urgency—a need for each guy to claim a woman and hook up. Other groups are closed off and uptight. But this group, this table, looks like a hell of a good time.

I sigh and meet Mia's eyes. She smirks, as if she knows exactly what I'm thinking.

Before any of us can plan how to approach their table, our server comes over with a bottle of champagne nestled into an ice bucket.

"From the gentlemen in the corner," she explains, pointing over her shoulder.

I look up and my eyes meet his again. This time, his look is more pointed. More...knowing.

I grin, he returns the smile, and my confidence grows.

The server pops the bottle and pours us each a glass.

I lift it in his direction, and tilt my head, asking, *Are you coming over or what?*

He chuckles and narrows his eyes for a long moment before standing. He takes his beer, walking toward me slowly.

Izzy sucks in a sharp breath. "Get it, girl," she murmurs.

I dip my head in a subtle nod. I am. I take a sip of my bubbly.

And by the time the handsome man with the bluest eyes I've ever seen stops in front of me, I'm well on my way to being tipsy. A bit from the alcohol and a bit from his presence.

"Hey," he says, holding out his hand. "I'm Leif."

Leif. I've never heard that name before, but I like it. I like names, people, and things that are different.

I shake his hand. "Cami. Thank you for the champagne."

The girls echo their thanks, and he smiles and nods at each of them.

"What are you celebrating?" he asks, dropping an elbow to the high-top table we're seated at.

"Graduation!" Tamara informs him.

Surprise ripples over his expression. "From university?"

"Of Minnesota," I share.

He rears back slightly, his eyes widening. "I'm from Minnesota."

I grin. "Small world."

"Guess so," he agrees, glancing at his friends.

Slowly, they make their way to our table too.

"Are all of you Minnesotans?" Mia asks.

"Fuck no," one of the guys laughs. "I'm Chris."

"We're celebrating his bachelor party," Leif explains.

"Congrats!" I say enthusiastically.

"When's the big day?" Tamara asks.

"July 28," Chris replies, grinning.

"This is Hudson, James, and Ray," Leif introduces his other friends.

"Good to meet you," Mia replies, gesturing for the guys to take a seat or pull up a barstool.

The men exchange a look—it only takes a second—before they agree to join our table.

A new tray of shots is delivered.

Leif shifts his stool and given how many bodies are now seated around the high-top, his thigh presses into mine. A strong, muscled leg, covered in denim. It's rough against my bare skin and surprisingly intimate since it shouldn't even register on my radar.

But it does. He does.

"So, you're celebrating?" Leif asks.

"As are you," I remind him, tipping my glass in his direction.

He clinks his glass against mine, amusement, curiosity, and something deeper—desire?—rolling through his irises. "What are the odds I'd meet a fellow Minnesotan—a fellow alumnus from U of M—here?"

I bite my bottom lip. "It's fate."

"Kismet," he agrees before we both toss back our shots.

Destiny.

If you believe in those types of things.

TWO

Leif

"Wait! You live in Ottawa?" Mia points at Hudson.

He smirks. "Yep. Leif used to be my roommate before he moved."

"And you're from...Honey Harbor?" Mia's forehead wrinkles as she tries to remember where Chris is from. "In Upstate New York."

"Yes," he confirms.

"And you're Minnesotan." Mia gestures toward me.

"Texas," Ray provides his home state.

"Jersey," James tacks on.

Tamara shakes her head. "How do y'all know each other?"

I snort. "College. Same as you."

"Wait! You all went to U of M too?" Mia gushes.

"Sure did," Ray confirms.

"Oh my God! It's like an alumni reunion." Mia's wide eyes meet Cami's. "That's what we are now! Alumni!"

"Cut her off," Izzy mutters, flicking her hand in front of her face.

Cami reaches for Mia's margarita and takes a sip before her friend grabs it back. She winks at me playfully and I'm pinned in place by her blue eyes. Damn, but she's gorgeous. Simultaneously inviting yet enigmatic. She's got this pull to her—an energy that hums just under the surface. I want to get tugged into her orbit, even though I have no clue what it will entail. I fight my grin; sure looks like fun though.

One side of her mouth lifts in response and I can't help but fully smile. There's that hint of intrigue I want to understand. With light brown hair that hangs past her shoulders, soft bangs—*Birkin bangs*! My sister Annie's voice echoes in my eardrums—and dazzling blue eyes, Cami is obviously beautiful, but it's more than that. And the more is the thing I can't put my finger on.

I like the sound of her laugh and the easy way she carries herself. Like she doesn't take herself—or anyone else—too seriously. My family says I'm like that too. And I am, to an extent. But I also only do shit on my own terms.

"What are you doing now that you're finished with school?" I ask her, more interested than I usually am about a woman I just met.

She sighs and sweeps her bangs to the side, out of her eyes. "Actually, I'm moving. Next week."

I arch an eyebrow. "New job?"

She wrinkles her nose. "At an accounting firm. It's an entry-level position, a year to learn the ropes before taking the CPA exam."

I chuckle. "Is that what you majored in? Accounting?"

Cami nods. Then shrugs. "My parents thought it would be a stable career path for me."

"Uh-huh," I agree, narrowing my eyes. "And do you always do what your parents want?" I mean it to sound teasing. Playful. Instead, it comes out with a thread of judgment.

Cami rears back and I mentally swear at myself.

Then, she catches me off guard by laughing. "Honestly? More than I'd like to admit."

I smile back. I like that she can laugh it off. Roll with it.

"But I went rogue," she lowers her voice.

I arch an eyebrow, waiting.

"I minored in drawing and painting."

I tip my head back and laugh. I like that she's got some spunk. A dash of sass. "So, where are you headed?" I ask, steering our conversation.

"Tennessee." Her eyes light up at she says it. At least this part, she's excited about.

I shake my head. "You're kidding me? Nashville?"

"Nope. Knoxville." She must note the change in my expression because she tacks on, "Why?"

I stare at her. There's no way she knows...right? I was traded to the Tennessee Thunderbolts about six months ago, and while hockey fans and enthusiasts know this information, Cami hasn't given the slightest clue that she recognizes me as an NHL player.

"I live there," I reply. "Actually, I recently moved there too—about six months ago."

Her eyes widen and her mouth pops open. Then, another stream of that infectious laughter. "Seriously? That's amazing! We'll need to keep in touch." She whips out her phone and passes it to me. "Here. Give me your number. I'll hit you up when I'm all settled."

Behind Cami, I see Hudson trying to hide his laughter. He gives me a look.

Cami has no fucking clue who I am. And I love that about her. About this night.

When was the last time a woman asked for my number in a nonchalant—almost dismissive—way?

Years. It's been years.

Because now, women clamor for my number and then call incessantly. They all want one thing—access. Access to a person, a socioeconomic level, a professional connection, or a social scene. It's gotten so out of hand that I rarely give out my personal number.

But for this woman...

I have no idea why, but I program my cell number under the contact name Tennessee and call myself so I'll have her number too.

She laughs when she sees that I saved my number under the name of the state. Rolling her eyes, she mutters, "I like that you know I've got prospects lined up in different area codes."

I chuckle.

"You can save me under Knoxville," she advises. "It's my new chapter so... I'm ready to shed Minneapolis as my identifier."

I snort. "You got it, babe." I save her under her preferred location, and we toss back another shot.

Hell, it's easy. Funny.

Thrilling.

And the night is still early.

FROM THE ROOFTOP PATIO, we move to dinner. It was supposed to be a guy's dinner, to celebrate Chris. But with James and Ray hitting it off with Mia and Tamara, and

Izzy being an easy conversationalist, Chris changes the reservation without any input from us.

James smacks him on the back in thanks.

Chris is a good guy like that. He's been with Casey since high school, but he's always been a solid wingman. He and Casey have one of those relationships we all aspire to have— one where they're each other's biggest supporters. One where they are truly best friends, probably because they grew up together.

"Okay, hang on a second," Chris says as we near the entrance to the steakhouse we're dining at. "I need a photo for Casey."

"Aw, she sounds awesome," Izzy says, huddling in between her friends.

"She's the best," Ray admits, meaning it.

We take a group shot and Chris sends it to Casey.

He smirks and flashes me the screen so I can read their text thread.

> Chris: (Photo)

> Chris: Dinner plans have changed. Look at Ray.

> Casey: OMG! He's got his arm around her...

> Casey: This is very forward for him.

I snort. Ray is one of the most direct, least subtle men I know, especially when it comes to a woman he's trying to impress.

> Casey: I spy Leif with his arm around that hot brunette.

> **Chris:** Cami—she's moving to Knoxville next week.

> **Casey:** Staaaaahp! Need all the details.
> Enjoy dinner and have fun with your crew.
> Love you.

> **Chris:** I love you, Case. Call you later.

A ball wedges itself in my throat as Chris tucks his phone back into his pocket and grips my shoulder. He's been in love with Casey for years and I couldn't be happier that they're tying the knot. But over the past year, my brothers Kingston, Jakob, and Jensen have all met and settled down with their soul mates.

It's starting to feel like I'm being left behind and, if I aspire to have what Chris and my brothers share with their women, I may be behind forever.

Man, we used to bust Chris's balls for being so damn into Casey. And now... I shake my head. It's the type of trust, the same level of respect, I've witnessed between my parents my entire life.

It's the kind of shit I never thought I'd care about and with each passing year, I want it more. Not necessarily the steps—the marriage and the house, the dog and the flower beds—but the person. The one I can count on and confide in. Be honest with. Spend an entire lazy Sunday wrapped up in her world and not feel claustrophobic at the end of it.

We enter the steakhouse and follow the hostess to our table.

I slide into the chair beside Cami's and catch her eye. She looks hesitant, almost...worried. Dipping my head toward her, I ask, "What is it?"

"Are you sure this is okay?" Her eyes dart around the table, settling an extra beat on Chris. "We don't want to crash his night or ruin your plans or anything."

I smirk and shake my head, palming the back of her chair. Even with a couple inches between my fingertips and her back, I can feel the heat of her body. Unable to stop myself, I brush my fingertips over the silky strands of her hair as I lean closer. "Nah, it's fine. Chris and Casey have been together forever. He didn't even want a bachelor party, but Casey insisted he do something fun. She called Hudson and me and demanded we take him somewhere." I chuckle. "Not that we wouldn't have planned a trip anyway. But he's cool to just have dinner, toss back a few drinks, and hang out." As I say the words, I realize the truth behind them.

For Chris and Hudson, this weekend is a chill time. For me, Ray, and James, it's an opportunity to drink too much and hook up with random women.

I glance at Chris, nodding along with whatever Hudson is saying. They're perfectly content to step back as their friends try to connect with these beautiful women we just met. They're in the same world that King, Jake, and Jensen are. Will I ever get to that place? Will I ever find a woman I want to be rooted next to?

"You sure?" Cami asks, turning her neck to face me fully. Her mouth purses like a rosebud and she has a tiny freckle above her top lip, on the right side.

"Absolutely," I promise.

She bites her bottom lip and a slight blush works over her cheeks. As the wine is poured and dinner is ordered, that blush deepens.

She speaks more freely. I laugh more often.

And by the time Hudson picks up the bill, I've got my

hand resting on Cami's thigh underneath the table, her shoulder is leaning into my side, and I've never felt more excited about the stretch of hours before us.

For me, tonight is just beginning, and I want all the time I can get with this mysterious woman with the infectious smile.

THREE

Cami

It's ethereal. That moment at a club, in a crowd, where the bodies of everyone pressing around you, the pulse of the beat, hell, even the particles of air, seem to pause. They slow from a frenetic discord to a gentle heartbeat. Steady.

Leif and I share that moment.

His fingers are twisted in the material of my shirt and he's fisting it in his right hand, pulling my body closer as we dance, grind, together. I've got one hand gripping his hip, the other resting on the swell of his shoulder. Sweat drips down my spine from hours of dancing. I tossed my hair up in a bun hours ago. My body feels electric, like one touch from him in the right spot, and I'll short-circuit.

I'm breathless and drunk on his presence. Well, that and the shots I consumed since dinner. But it feels good. God, it feels right.

And then, we have the moment.

I don't think I've ever had the moment before. Not even

with Levi. No, everything with Levi was a blur of high highs and low lows. In hindsight, Mom was onto something when she accused me of making a series of poor judgment calls. Decisions I have to live with.

When Leif's eyes meet mine, the guilt and shame I harbor evaporates. I'm not naïve Cami. I'm me again—what you see is what you get.

Leif's eyes widen slightly, appearing just as startled as I feel, before the outer rings of that mesmerizing blue darken from the color of the Caribbean to the shade of the Mediterranean.

My fingernails dig into his shoulder and my back arches on its own accord. He draws me closer—how is that even possible?

The sound of the music fades. The person who bumps into me—Izzy or Tamara—from behind doesn't fully register.

The back of Leif's hand drags up the side of my body. Slowly. Sensually. My eyes close as his knuckles glide over my cheek. He tucks a tendril of hair behind my ear, his thumb pressing against my earlobe.

And when I open my eyes, he's looking at me intently. His eyebrows are pulled together, a tiny line forming between them. His eyes study me carefully, like a treasure, like I'm the most beautiful woman he's ever seen. His lips part and he releases a long exhale as his fingers skate across my face and his thumb lands in the center of my chin. He shakes his head slightly, as if in awe, as if this is the most meaningful exchange he's ever experienced.

The look in his eyes, the honest emotion stamped in his expression, crashes over me like a tidal wave. My hand presses to his, our fingers linking together, as he cradles my face.

He's not looking at me like I let him down. A hot mess.

He's not shaking his head like I'm a silly girl who read the situation wrong.

Or like this is a fun one-night-whatever that won't matter tomorrow.

His electric blue eyes bore into mine like they're seeing straight to my soul. And they're not scared. Or frustrated.

They're hopeful, reflecting a prism of possibilities.

They're honest, pouring out as much of his emotions as they take in of mine.

They're enchanted. *I enchant him.*

He blinks once and then, in that slow motion way of the best romance movies I've ever watched, his mouth arcs over mine. I lift my chin, waiting and wanting for the gift he's about to bestow.

And he misses his mark. Someone slams into Leif from behind and he stumbles forward, stepping on my toe and smacking his mouth against my ear.

He drags me with him, one strong arm banding across my lower back.

His eyes are wide—startled—as his other hand grips my shoulder. "Cami!" His eyes fly over my face. "Are you okay? Did I hurt you?"

"Just my toes," I admit, feeling the stomp of his foot reverberate through my body.

"Shit!" He moves to drop to his knees, but I clasp his shoulders and keep him upright.

"No, it's okay," I assure him. "I'm fine."

He whirls around, keeping one hand on my hip and tucking me behind his large frame.

Oh, no. My nerves scatter and my senses go on high alert. I've been in this position too many times with Levi. This is the part where the guy loses his mind and—

"You okay, dude?" Leif asks the man who bumped into him.

Um, what? I press up on my tippy toes to get a better view and wince at the pain that travels through my left foot.

"I fucking love this song!" The guy is wasted and stumbling. He grins crookedly at Leif, and nods his head to the beat, completely unaware that he nearly took us out.

Leif places a hand on his shoulder and leans forward, saying something to the man. The man points to some friends and Leif gestures them over. He speaks to them, but I can't catch his words. The friends seem receptive, and I watch as Leif hands them some cash. Then, they usher their friend away.

Leif turns back around to face me. "How's your foot? Do you need ice?"

"What was that?" I point toward the group of men.

Leif follows my gaze and shrugs. "That guy was hammered. I just want to make sure he gets some water in his system and takes it easy. He could get himself jammed up if he's not careful." Leif looks around the club and I note the swarm of dancing bodies. "Things always tend to go sideways at this time of night."

"Yeah," I laugh, staring at him. Who the hell is this guy? Any man I know would have decked the dude for pushing us, or, at the very least, exchanged some heated words. Levi would have knocked him out completely.

"You sure you're okay?" Leif asks, his lips brushing over the shell of my ear.

I nod, pulling back to stare at him. He looks worried— genuinely concerned for my well-being. Not defensive, needing to protect his ego. Not angry, that a stranger ruined his chance to kiss me. Just...sincere.

As much as I hate that I compare him to Levi, in this

moment, I'm relieved that I'm attracted to a man so different than the mercurial musician. Right now, I want to press myself against the considerate, laid-back, thoughtful man in front of me and kiss him hard.

Placing my palms on his cheeks, I lean into Leif, go up on my tippy toes, and kiss him passionately.

When my lips meet his, my body implodes, and I cling to him. Physically, my restraint started slipping the second I laid eyes on him. But emotionally? Leif just proved he's a man worth connecting with and any reasons I had to hold back disappear. My hands track his back; his hands grip my waist.

We come together like a tornado spiraling amid a hurricane and the sound of the club rushes around us, pulling us into the vortex and pulsing in my eardrums.

My arms wind around Leif's neck. He sweeps me into his arms, palming my ass like he can't control himself for a second longer.

Our tongues duel and twist. Our hands touch and memorize. But it's not slow and sensual now, no, it's borderline frantic.

"Fuck, Cami. You're something else," Leif pants in my ear.

I chuckle but the sound is too high. Reedy. "I don't want tonight to end, Leif."

He pulls back slightly to give me a look. "We've got hours ahead of us, beautiful."

I nearly shudder at the promise in his words. Hours? Yes, please. I want all of them. "Promise?" I taunt.

He grins, a quick flash. "Cross my fucking heart." He tosses his gesture from earlier back at me.

I smile. I like that we have...what? An inside joke? It's silly and childish yet it lights me up like a Christmas tree.

"Stay with me, tonight," he says—he's not asking.

And I like that too.

"I'm all yours." I arch into him again, pressing my breasts into his chest. God, it's been a long time since I've felt this confident with a man. This...honest about my own wants.

He grabs a handful of my ass and squeezes. "Want to get out of here?"

"I do," I admit, glancing around to find my friends.

Luckily, they're not far away and when I meet Izzy's eyes and gesture that I'm leaving with Leif, she arches one eyebrow. I roll my eyes, and she snorts and gives a little wave.

"What was that?" Leif laughs, catching our exchange.

"That was me telling Izzy we're out, her asking me if I'm sure, me saying 'seriously,' and her laughing."

"You had that whole conversation with one look?" he questions, lacing his fingers with mine and moving us toward the exit.

"We've been friends forever," I shout over the music. "Don't you need to find your friends?"

"I'll text them," he replies as we weave through bodies.

We get our things from the VIP booth. Leif sees Ray and passes him a wad of bills for tonight's fun, and we leave the club.

When we get outside, the fresh air slams into us. Even though it's hot and humid, it feels refreshing after hours in the club.

We stall for a second as Leif looks me over. "You okay?"

I nod, smirking. I like that he checks in. Most guys I know aren't this attentive. "I'm good. Where to?"

Leif shrugs and glances down the street. "Actually, there's a place I've been meaning to pass by. It's a two-minute walk." He eyes my shoes, my poor foot that took the brunt of his weight, and again, his concern causes a warmth to spread through my limbs.

I slip my hand into Leif's. Right now, I don't feel the pain in my foot. I don't feel anything but anticipation for the hours ahead. "Lead the way."

We take off at a stroll. A casual, familiar walk at midnight in Vegas. It's not desperate. We're definitely drunk but we're not falling over each other, unable to function.

Instead, our conversation is easy. Our silence, comfortable.

It's fucking unnerving, that's what it is. And I relish it.

When we arrive at our destination, Leif knocks twice on a nondescript door.

A thrill of nerves, of anticipation mixed with fear, runs up my spine.

Where are we? Did I read this situation wrong?

A night from Spain—Ibiza—comes buzzing back. Of Levi scoring drugs. Getting high.

I shake my head.

Shit, I should have shared my location with the girls.

I look up at Leif but he's as cool as he was a second ago.

The door opens.

"Yeah?" a gruff guy asks.

"I'm here for Skip," Leif explains.

The guy gives Leif a long look before he swears under his breath. "You coming now?"

Leif shrugs. "Was in the area." He tosses me a wink, like I'm in on the secret.

What the hell is the secret?

And why, with my track record, am I so desperate to be in on it?

"You ready?" Leif squeezes my fingers.

I look up at him. Fear, excitement, desire flooding my senses.

Where the hell are we? Am I really going to follow a man I just met through a random, unmarked door in Vegas?

For a heartbeat, that night from Barcelona, the one that changed the course of my life, reverberates in my mind. Levi and the cocaine and the pictures... I shake my head.

Leif waits for my response. He doesn't rush me. He doesn't say anything. He just stares at me with those mesmerizing eyes and pure patience. Like he would wait all night.

"Sure," I say, taking a leap of faith.

Then, Leif leads me through the door, and it closes behind us.

We move through a heavy curtain into another area. My heart gallops and I pinch Leif's fingers. Sensing my unease, he wraps his arm around my waist, banding me to his side.

When we emerge on the other side of the curtain, the bright light assaults my eyes and I blink rapidly.

A buzzing sound rattles in my eardrums. I look around.

"This is a tattoo parlor!" I announce.

Leif smirks. "Yeah. I know it's not conventional, but Marco mixes a good fucking cocktail." He flips his chin toward a guy behind a bar, concocting something in a shaker. Two women and a man hang out in front of the bar, talking casually. "And I've been meaning to roll through." Leif bumps his shoulder against mine. "Thanks for doing this with me."

"Of course," I say. *What the fuck are we doing?* I do not voice that.

"Laid-back Leif," a large dude says, moving toward us.

Leif drops his hold on my fingers to do some bromance shake with this large, towering man. "What's good, Skip?"

Skip shakes his head and laughs. "Hey, little mama." He holds out his fist to me.

I pound it.

"You getting a piece tonight, too?" Skip asks me.

"I, um, say that again?" I try to process his question.

Skips laughs, while Leif grins and wraps that strong arm around me again.

I try not to be too obvious as I melt into his side.

"Nah, tonight, I want to finish mine," Leif explains.

Skip guffaws. "Tonight? I love how you think I'd have nothing else going on."

Leif glances around the chill space. Turns back toward Skip. "Can you fit me in, Skippy?"

Skip flashes him the middle finger. "Don't fucking call me peanut butter."

I grin. Leif laughs.

"And I always got time for you, you fucker," Skip continues, turning toward his station.

Leif and I follow and Leif leans against the tattoo table.

"Wait, you're getting a tattoo?" I ask.

Skip snorts and Leif's grin widens. He pulls off his shirt and I inhale sharply. Jesus, the man is all muscle!

His shoulders are broad and strong. His pecs could do a damn dance. His abs comprise a literal washboard. Corded ropes for veins in those strong forearms. But his back, his back makes me audibly groan.

"You like it?" He glances at me over his shoulder as I study his tattoo.

It isn't finished yet but... "It's glorious." The words tumble from my mouth.

Skip points at me. "I like you, little mama."

"It's where I feel the most at peace," Leif admits quietly.

My eyes flick up from the work on his back—a cresting wave, a surfboard adrift, a brilliant sunset—to his face. He's staring at me like he's holding his breath. Like this is some sort of test and he's waiting to see if I pass.

"Like you can block out all the noise and just be," I murmur.

Surprise, quickly followed by gratitude, flares in his irises. "Exactly. You got something like that, Cam?"

I nod slowly. Obviously, my family knows I like to draw. Sketch. Fashion designs mostly. But they never took it seriously. It was a hobby I had until I had to buckle down and become an adult—study accounting.

But... "Yeah, I do," I tell Leif. Holding his gaze, I continue, "Drawing. That's my thing."

He watches me for a long beat before nodding once. "Your minor."

"Right." I bite my bottom lip, glancing around the tattoo parlor. Another night in Spain zips through my mind and I rub the side of my ribs where my first tattoo permanently marks my skin.

A reminder of that semester. A warning to never repeat it.

Skip grabs a stool and rolls over. Glancing between Leif and me, he chuckles under his breath and pulls up a stool for me.

I plop down and smile. "Want me to hold your hand, Leif?"

At that, Skip throws his head back and laughs. "Little mama, fuck, girl, you gotta let me do your next tattoo."

Leif's laughing too and then, he sobers. "Wait, Cami, you got any ink?"

Grinning, I nod. Thank God Mom doesn't know—she would literally go into cardiac arrest.

Leif and Skip exchange a look.

I start to roll up the flimsy material of my shirt and Leif sits up straighter, his expression darting from me to Skip and back again. A protective glint flares in his eyes and I pause. "It's along my ribs."

"Damn, that hurts," Skip mutters, leaning closer to read the words. "*Sogno con gli occhi aperti.*"

Leif looks at me, his expression bathed in curiosity.

"I dream with open eyes," I explain.

Skip shakes his head. "That's deep, little mama."

I snort. "It was supposed to be in Spanish since I got it in Spain, but I messed up Google translate and got it in Italian."

Skip laughs and Leif chuckles but his expression searches mine. Again, it's as though he can see below the surface. Deeper.

Skip gets to work, and Leif takes my hand, surprising us both.

He winks at me, and something shifts between us.

We have another moment.

A real one.

One that changes everything and makes me wish this moment, this night, this man at my side, could be my forever.

FOUR

Leif

She got a freaking tattoo.

Better than that? She drew it. One for me and one for her.

That alone makes this ink more special—it's a bond we share.

I keep running my thumb over the bandage on her wrist.

She grins at me, shaking her bangs out of her eyes.

"I can't believe you got a tattoo," I tell her what I'm thinking. She snorts. "You did, too!"

"Skip's been working on that piece for months. Every time I'm in Vegas, I roll through," I remind her. When I first pushed into Skip's studio with Cami at my side, I figured she'd balk. A small part of me wished she did.

I wanted her to react to my taking her somewhere random—to a place that wasn't solely for a hookup. To a place I never take women because my tattoos are sacred to me.

So yeah, a part of me wanted her to push back on the tattoo parlor because letting her in and having her embrace it is a head trip I'm not ready to dissect.

I'm a chill guy. I go with the flow. Hence my nickname—Laid-back Leif.

But Cami? Cami is next-fucking-level cool.

She fingers the bandage on my inner wrist. The tattoo she drew for us. "And this one?"

I chuckle. She's right. "You regret it?" I hope she doesn't. But, getting a matching tattoo with a stranger on a whim isn't something most women I know would be okay with. Hell, if my sister pulled shit like this, my brothers and I would have something to say about it!

Her eyes are navy when they meet mine. "Not even a little bit."

My smile widens and I tuck this gorgeous woman underneath my arm. It's late and yet, I'm not ready to turn in. I could walk the streets, just talking with her, until the sun rises. And I'd relish it.

The cocktails Marco concocted have pushed me from tipsy to drunk and it feels good. I'm fucking coasting and I like doing it with a woman I want to learn more about.

"Tell me something no one knows about you," I say as we cross the street.

She looks up, and those bangs fall into her wide eyes. She's quiet for a long moment. We get to the other side of the street and keep walking. Vegas is still busy at this time of morning but since we're not in the heart of things, the crowd's thinned out.

I think she's going to brush off my question but then she announces, "I really don't want to be an accountant."

"Seriously?" I frown. "Then why are you moving your

life across the country? I mean, for a job you don't really want?"

She shrugs. "I lied. I guess people—my sister Jenna, Izzy and the girls—know I don't really want to be an accountant. It's what my parents want for me. A steady, reliable career path. The part no one knows is I took the job because I need space from my family. I want distance. I want hundreds of miles in between us so I can... I don't know. Breathe," she tacks on, the word coming out on an exhale.

I hold her closer, understanding immediately what she's talking about. "Want to let the pressure leak out a little," I surmise, recalling how my dad pushed my brothers and me in hockey. Hockey always came first and even though deep down, I know he would have supported an alternative career choice, especially under Mom's guidance, the fact that my brothers and I all play in the NHL isn't exactly a coincidence. It's motivated by expectation.

"Exactly." Cami gives me a soft smile. "Tell me something no one knows."

I snort and dip my head in agreement. A truth for a truth. "I have a big family and I've always been known as the chill, laid-back, go-with-the-flow guy."

"Yeah," Cami notes, glancing up at me. "I was surprised when you helped that drunk guy instead of getting into it with him."

I chuckle. "Would fighting with him help the situation at all?"

"Nope."

"Exactly."

"But most guys would have felt the need to show off. Especially in front of a woman," she continues. And she's right, most guys would.

But... "I'm not most guys."

"I'm picking up on that," she admits. "You're laid-back..." Cami reminds me of my original line of thought.

"I am." I glance down at her. "But what if I don't want to be? Or what if I'm only seen that way because nothing—no one—has ever mattered enough to lose it over?"

Cami slows her pace and touches my wrist gently. Encouragingly.

"I nearly got expelled from college and cost a professor her job," I admit. Her eyes lighten, curious. I sigh. "We were hooking up on the down-low. It was casual. Fun, I guess, because it was forbidden. But when it came time to deal with the consequences, she was gutted, and I was...apathetic. If I got expelled, I got expelled." My jaw tightens as I admit it. "I don't know why I'm telling you this."

"Because I asked," Cami says simply, without a shred of judgment. Instead, she's looking at me with compassion—with understanding—I don't deserve.

I take her hand and squeeze her fingers. "I want something real enough—something that matters with someone I care about—so I can be more than just Laid-back Leif."

Cami nods slowly. "I get that. Sometimes, the labels we had in the past follow us into the present."

"Yeah," I agree. "Exactly."

Cami sighs. "I was seen as impulsive and even a little reckless in high school. That followed me into college, and I was okay with it. In fact, I liked how others viewed my spontaneity. But my parents hated it. They worried—for good reason—and even though I've reined it in, and I'm not nearly as wild as I once was, my mom still views me as her carefree daughter who needs looking after."

I smirk, swinging our joined hands between us as we walk down the street. This, right here with her, feels natural.

Honest in a way I crave. "So, you're moving to Tennessee to be an accountant?"

"Yeah." She wrinkles her nose. "But let's not talk about boring work."

"Okay. What do you want to talk about?"

Her eyes dance as she gazes up at me. "If you want to change the way people see you, what do you want them to see instead of your laid-back nickname?"

"Ooh, tough question, Cam."

She shimmies her shoulders, proud of herself.

"I guess a guy who is committed. Dedicated. Determined." My dad pops into my mind and I chuckle. "To be honest, I'm partly describing my father and even though I don't want to be as serious as he is, I look up to him. I want to be that stand-up guy that people know they can rely on. I want to have kids who trust me the same way I trust him."

"You want to be a dad?" Her voice is soft.

"Hell yeah," I laugh. "I want a ton of kids. I want to teach them how to surf. How to skate and swim. How to read. I want to go on epic trips and see a slice of the world through their eyes." I grin at her. "I love being around kids."

"I do, too," she admits. "But most men I know don't talk about fatherhood."

Again, "I'm not most—"

"Guys," she supplies. "You're not." She bites her bottom lip and looks up at me, studying my expression. "You're a million times better," she breathes out, but her gaze is serious.

"I like the way you see me. Right now," I admit, not caring how dumb I sound. Cami is looking at me like I could be more than a guy she hooks up with in Vegas. Her expression is wide open—stamped with the same vulnerability that I'm openly sharing. And I don't want to lose that. This moment with her, it snaps things into place like a puzzle. I can see the big picture and the pieces I've been missing. Right now, it's as though she could help fill those holes.

"I like the guy you are, Leif. And I like the man you want to become. I get what you're saying. You want something with stakes," she explains.

"Yeah," I snort, relieved that she gets it. "I want stakes."

Cami nods slowly. Her eyes catch on something, and she grins. "How badly?"

"What?" I laugh.

"How badly do you want stakes? We could do something wild."

"Wild?" I release her hand to hold up my wrist. "Wilder than getting matching tattoos? This ink is permanent, babe. You and me—we're marked together for life."

"Yeah," she agrees, taking my hand again and tugging me toward her destination. "We could up the ante."

I laugh. "What game are we betting on?"

She rolls her lips together, that sparkle in her eyes bright and tempting. "Game of life, Leif."

"What?" I snort, letting her drag me to...a fucking chapel.

"Leif." Cami spins to look at me. Her smile is big and blinding. Excitement dances in her eyes and the hopeful anticipation in her expression hits me right in the chest. "Will you marry me?"

Fuck. My heartbeat kicks behind my breastbone and my ability to breathe short-circuits. This incredible woman— smart, sexy, and so damn enthusiastic—is looking at me like she sees me.

Me. Leif Bang.

Not the hockey player. Not the screwup. Not the fun dude down to shred waves or funnel a beer.

Me. With all the parts no one takes the time to get to know. The parts no one cares about.

A flicker of nerves zips over her expression and before she can voice it—before she can rescind her brave offer—I step forward and take her hand. "It'd be a goddamn honor, Cami."

She smiles shyly and it steals my breath.

"Hey, is that your full name?"

She rolls her lips together. "It's Camille."

"Camille. That's beautiful."

Her smile widens. "Thank you. Are you sure about this?"

I smirk and glance at the chapel behind her. "Are you sure, babe? I don't want you to have any regrets. Ever." As I say the words, I realize I mean them. I'd hate for her to look back and wish she did something differently. Maybe that's why I hate the thought of her crunching numbers in a fucking cubicle when she could be out in the world, creating art and inspiring strangers.

"I never have regrets," she assures me. "Not anymore." She taps her ribs where her first tattoo is scrawled. "Open eyes, remember?"

I pause for a beat, wondering what happened in her past to make her state a claim so boldly. Yet, for some strange reason, I believe her. I mean, we barely know each other and yet, there's a connection between us. Something deeper than a random night out. Something more meaningful than a series of tequila shots and general conversation.

I get her; she sees me. And right now, we're standing in front of an adorable chapel, and I fucking *want* to call her my wife. Because men like me don't meet women like Cami.

"There's a lot you don't know about me," I tell her. Now would be the opening to admit I'm a hockey player. But, why? She asked *me* to marry her, not the NHL persona people clamor around. *Me.*

"I know enough."

"I don't have a ring."

She shrugs. "Don't need one."

I shake my head. "Yeah, you do." I give her fingers a little squeeze and drop her hand. "Give me two minutes. Don't move." I point at her.

"Where are you going?"

"Don't you move, Camille," I call over my shoulder as I jog back across the street. I make quick work of slipping into the gas station, and eyeing one of those old-fashioned gumball machines that never spits out gumballs. Instead, it's a handful of Skittles or a small egg with a random surprise in it.

"Hey dude, can I get change?" I hand the cashier a twenty-dollar bill.

He doesn't even bat an eye. Another night in Vegas, I guess.

He hands me rolls of quarters and I shove some into the machine, turning the dial until a small plastic egg pops out. It's a little bear. I try again. A dinosaur. Nope.

On the seventh try, I get it. A purple plastic princess ring with a glitter crown. I leave the other toys on the countertop. "Thanks, my man. Give these to some kid passing through!"

Then I run out of the gas station, cross the street, and skid to a stop in front of an amused Cami. "Mission accomplished."

She giggles and takes my hand, pulling me into the chapel.

But I'm not nervous. I know in my bones that this is the right call. This is having stakes and I fucking want them. Our night—our story—is still young and I'm not done collecting pieces of it with her.

"Hold up." I pause as I swipe some flowers from a table and pass them to Cami.

She's giddy, bouncing from one foot to the next. "Now, we're stealing?"

"Borrowing," I shush her.

"Let me freshen up." She indicates the women's bathroom.

"You look beautiful." I mean it too.

She smirks but enters the women's room.

While she's fixing her makeup, I make the necessary arrangements and pay for our marriage license. Then, I take a second to fix my hair and straighten my shirt.

I never really gave a shit about having a wedding; it was always the marriage I was more interested in. I've seen my dad quietly revere my mom in his own way—he's not showy or overly affectionate as much as he's steady and reliable—my entire life. He's never faltered in his support for her. He's never tried to tame her streak of wild or question her when she dives into a new project headfirst. The time she decided, on a whim, to remodel the guest bathroom or start a pie-making business come to mind. Not to mention this past year, when she traveled between my brothers' places, meddling in their lives and becoming a matchmaker. Dad has always been her rock.

And in turn, she loves him with every fiber of her being. She supported his career as an NHL player and now a juniors coach. Often, she would wake up at four thirty AM just to share a first cup of coffee with him, the two of them sitting at the kitchen table with their heads bent together, as the snow of a Minnesotan winter fell softly outside the window.

That's what I want. Deep down, I want the steady and the wild to come together and work. I want what my mom and dad have. Laid-back Leif would be laughed out of fucking town if anyone knew all those details. But I've already admitted it to Cami and she...asked me to marry her. I pull out my cell phone and text my brother, Jensen.

Me: I'm about to do something crazy.

He doesn't answer and I'm not surprised. Since he's fallen for his girlfriend, Hollywood sensation Bailey Walker, he's stopped spending late nights gaming and started spending them with her. I want that, too.

Slipping my phone into my pocket, I wait for Cami. She steps out of the bathroom and looks around nervously. As soon as her eyes latch on mine, she relaxes, smiles.

"You're like no one I've ever met," I tell her the truth. "Gorgeous. But it's more than skin deep."

"You're unexpected," she replies, her tone even. Her words are strong but her voice is soft, almost hesitant. "Exactly what I hoped for and nothing like I deserve."

Her words are cryptic but then again, so is she. It's part of her charm.

We enter the chapel and Cami sucks in a deep breath. I pause, turning toward her.

"I should kiss you before we do this," I decide, stepping closer.

Surprise colors her eyes. "We've kissed before," she reminds me.

"Not like this," I confess, needing to kiss her softly. Reverently. Not in a sweaty club on a dance floor. "You can still change your mind." I place a hand on the small of her back and pull her into my frame until her hips line up with my thighs.

"I won't," she promises, lifting her face.

I shrug one shoulder, feigning more casual than I feel. Then, I dip my head, take her mouth, and kiss her sweetly.

And then, fiercely. Protectively. Thoroughly.

My surroundings cease to exist. The world quiets.

And there's this fucking moment. When everything I ever wanted is right before me and I'm as desperate to claim it as I am terrified I'll lose it.

My one hand is pressed against Cami's cheek. Her arms are wrapped around my waist, clinging to me.

The minister clears his throat, and we break apart, turning to look at him. "That's for after you say I do," he jokes, pointing at us.

Cami giggles and I grin.

"See you at the altar?" I whisper.

She holds up the bouquet of flowers I swiped. "I'll be the girl in jeans."

I laugh, a genuine, boisterous laugh.

She blows me a kiss and shoos me away.

And I stride to the altar to wait for the woman who will become my wife.

Cami. Camille... Shit, what's her last name?

FIVE

Cami

I'm not much of a crier. Not like my sister Jenna. Or Izzy. But my eyes glisten as I walk down the aisle to Leif.

It's terrifying and exhilarating. It's not the wedding I imagined but right now I'm happy. Sometimes, the best thing you can do is trust your intuition.

For a long time, after Levi, I forgot how to do that. But not anymore. Not tonight.

I'm not supposed to feel this much for a man I just met. But tequila braces me with a different type of courage, and I stride toward the man looking at me like I hung the moon.

Nerves gather in the pit of my stomach. A thrill of excitement shimmies across my shoulders. When I reach his side, calmness sweeps through me.

The minister begins his speech but I'm looking into Leif's bottomless blue eyes, free-falling.

Leif's expression is more serious than I anticipated. He's not cracking up or making jokes. He's not high out of his mind and slurring. He's holding my hand and peering into my soul.

I shiver from the intensity of his gaze and his eyebrows draw together slightly, as if concerned. I squeeze his hand to let him know I'm good.

I mean, sure, I'm a little nervous. Excited. Giddy. But in the best way possible. Leif and I clicked on a level I want to live in. A long time ago, I made bold decisions and embraced moments. Then, I became too fearful to make another misstep that I stopped savoring opportunities when they were presented.

This is one I don't want to miss out on. I'm not fearful, I'm elated.

Truly, genuinely happy.

We say our vows with an honesty I feel deep in my bones. Our voices are clear, ringing out in the space between us with a finality that isn't scary. It doesn't make me feel trapped. Instead, it's freeing. Filled with possibilities.

When it's time to exchange rings, both sides of Leif's mouth curl into a brilliant smile as he slides the purple crown on my finger.

We both stare in disbelief when it's—"a perfect fit," I breathe out, as if it confirms the success of our marriage.

I wiggle my fingers, admiring my ring.

I probably shouldn't love the piece of plastic as much as I do but it feels like a treasure.

Then, I pull the ring I made Leif—a knock-off Rainbow Looms circle of tiny, multi-colored, plastic hair ties I had in my purse and fashioned together in the women's bathroom—from my pocket and roll it onto his finger.

He chuckles in disbelief, his eyes shining. "You're resourceful. I like that."

"I now pronounce you husband and wife. You may kiss the bride," the minister concludes.

Leif arches an eyebrow and shuffles closer.

My breath hitches as he bends his strong body over mine. And I bow into him, knowing he won't break me, knowing he'll shield me. How the hell do I know that?

Before I can figure it out, my thoughts scatter.

Because Leif kisses me, and it's filled with awe. Reverence. A brand of something I've never tasted before, and I don't want to lose.

When he pulls back, our eyes hold for a long moment. Promises are made. Commitments are created. Trust, established.

"Do you want a picture?" the minister asks, interrupting our moment.

"Hell yes," I gush, passing him my phone.

Leif and I pose like goofballs, smiling or making silly faces for a few snaps before Leif swings me up in his arms, holds me tightly against his chest, and strides back down the aisle.

I giggle. "Are you seriously going to carry me back to the hotel?" My hotel is at least a twenty-minute walk from here.

"I am," he declares, stepping out into the early morning. "My hotel is on this street. And I can't wait to get you alone." He glances down at me and grins wolfishly. "Wife."

Wife. I shiver from that word in that tone.

At the severity of Leif's jaw, the strength of his arms holding me up, the quickness of his stride, I know he's experiencing the same impatient need that's circulating in my bloodstream.

"You know, we didn't have to get married to have sex," I joke lightly as we enter the lobby of his hotel. I glance around quickly but no one is paying attention to us. This is hardly an interesting scene in a Vegas hotel at three in the morning.

Leif snorts and maneuvers my body weight to jab the button for the elevator. "This isn't just sex, Cam." His voice is low and rumbly. His eyes flash to mine. "And it's not just for tonight."

Oh my.

My cheeks heat, my guy grins, and the elevator—blessedly—arrives.

Everything after that is a blur.

The sound of Leif's hotel door closing behind us. The grandeur of his hotel suite wraps around us like a cocoon as I step out of my heels and stretch my toes in the soft rug in the living room. The both of us rattling off messages to our friends that we're fine—better than fine.

"The guys must be out or sleeping," he mutters when no one pops their heads into the common space to say hello.

And then, Leif's hand slips across the small of my back. I turn into his arms and wind my arms behind his neck.

"You ever been married before?" I whisper. Clearly my priorities are messed up because I should have asked him this earlier.

"Never," he swears.

And that little thrill in my limbs grows and dances.

Leif scoops me up and relocates us into his bedroom. He closes the door behind us and peels off my shirt. I lift my arms so he can remove it, toss it on the floor behind me.

I work the buttons on his shirt and push the fabric off those strong shoulders. My fingers trail down the ridges of his abdomen—an entire freaking mountain range. "You work out a lot."

He chuckles and pops the button on my jeans. "You have no idea."

My eyes lift to his. "Not yet. But I'm about to find out."
I'm about to get my world flipped upside down. But from this
night with Leif and all the nights that come after, with my
husband.

"Yeah, you are," he agrees. Then, his mouth is on mine,
his hands squeezing my waist.

I hitch forward into his frame and let his kiss swallow me
whole. I don't want to come up for reality. Or air. I want this
—all of this—with him.

Leif coaxes my body into submission like he knows it intimately. His touch unravels my senses. He kisses me in a way
that absolves my past sins and makes my future beam
brightly.

I'm putty in his capable hands. He tests the weight of my
breasts, lowers his mouth to my nipples, and gives them more
attention than any man has before. Kneading and pinching.
Licking and sucking.

He removes his pants and boxers in one shot and I literally gasp at the perfection of his body.

His eyes dart to mine at the sounds that fall from my
mouth but there's no more light humor. Everything has
turned serious between us.

He's my husband. I'm his wife. And tonight is our
wedding night.

There aren't rushed touches. There's savoring.

There's no clashing of teeth. There's tasting and sipping
and devouring.

Leif drops to his knees at the side of the bed and tugs my
legs, hooking them around his shoulders.

"Oh, God." I grip the bedsheet in anticipation. I'm
already wet for him. Hell, I think I have been since he walked
onto that patio rooftop. The nerves in my body are taut, the
need seeping out as arousal between my thighs.

"So fucking perfect," Leif murmurs, dragging the pads of two fingers through my folds.

I groan at his touch. It's more than good. It's centering.

He does it again. And again.

His fingers drag across my sex lazily as he studies me. His eyes hold mine and the look in his—so fucking sexy and surprisingly hopeful—is a salve to years of thoughtless, careless flings and silly, pointless one-night stands.

I shift under his gaze. I squirm from his slow touch. And just when I think I can't take anymore, he lowers his mouth and uses his tongue.

"Leif!" I cry out, tightening my thighs around his head. My hands twist the sheets.

He uses his palms to slide under my ass and lift it. He pulls me closer as his tongue begins to dance across my pussy. He's a fucking expert. The pace, the pressure, the intensity, it's too much.

Within seconds, my back arches off the bed. Every nerve ending I have is on fire, flames licking higher, faster, stronger and then—I combust. "Leif, oh God, Leif." My eyes are closed, my head tossed back.

And my guy? My guy slows his ministrations and helps me ride out the most intense, powerful, all-consuming orgasm of my life. I whimper as I come down and he strokes my inner thighs, his mouth continuing to press kisses across my over-sensitized flesh.

When my thighs loosen their hold, he moves up my body like a freaking panther. Slow, steady, and focused. I open my arms, he falls into them, and the kiss we share should be fucking illegal.

"I'm clean, Cam," he swears.

"Me too," I promise. "And I'm on the pill."

He nods, holding my gaze to make sure.

"I don't want anything between us," he says. "Not tonight. But is that what you want?"

Jesus, this man. This man and these words.

"I'm more than good with that." I widen my legs.

He settles between them on his next kiss; he pushes inside with one thrust. I see fucking stars. Because he's big, and so fucking hard.

"Hold on to me, baby," he instructs.

I grip his shoulders before sliding my hands around to his back. Leif begins to rock in and out before he sets a pace that has my thighs quaking and the tendons in his neck stretching.

He's beautiful. Glorious. I can hardly take my eyes off him.

He works me over so fucking good, I come again. And only after, does he let himself lose control. He pounds into me, shifting from sensual to downright desperate. And then, he breaks apart and it's beautiful.

"Camille..." my full name on his lips. A shudder rolls through my limbs. The strength of his body seeps out in release, in need, in naked emotions that flit across his face. "Fuck, baby."

He collapses onto me and rolls to his side, taking me with him. I hold his face against my chest, stroking his hair and kissing his forehead. We're still joined together and I don't want to move. I don't even care that his semen leaks onto my inner thighs. I don't give a shit about the sticky mess we're making.

I just want this.

Another moment.

Another heartbeat.

Another kiss.

AT SOME POINT, I doze off. But when I wake in the morning, I do so with fucking panic.

The first thing that greets my eyes is the sexiest man I've ever had. Leif. And that's saying something because women across the country would sell their eggs for a night with Levi Rousell.

But Levi's got nothing on Leif. At least, not when I knew him—high, strung out, and on the brink of rehab.

I move to slip out from Leif's hold so I can use the bathroom and my eyes snag on the purple glitter crown ring on my finger.

"Oh, fuck," I mutter as the night before comes rushing back.

My head pounds and my throat feels dry enough to crack.

"I got fucking married," I recall, my thoughts hazy.

But my body isn't confused. It feels wonderful. Sated. Fulfilled.

Gah!

Still, I need to get the hell out of here.

Mom is going to kill me. How many times post-Levi and the pictures debacle did she warn me against getting caught up in nights like this? In morning-afters like the one I'm currently living? This is the stuff she tells me I need to think through.

But last night, I wasn't thinking as much as I was feeling. And it felt right. It felt good.

I felt like myself again.

I pull in a deep breath and let out a long exhale. I force myself to lie perfectly still and splay my hands wide on the bedsheet. I need to *think*.

Last night was...magic.

I cast another look at Leif. But damn did he make me feel good. Whole. Right.

I shake my head and wince at the sudden movement.

Who am I kidding? Who the hell meets a stranger in Vegas and thinks they're going to complete them?

My phone buzzes on the nightstand and I roll over to grab it before it can wake Leif.

Mom: Las Vegas, Cami? Are you serious?

Shit. I sigh heavily. My sister Jenna must have cracked. Knowing how relentless Mom can be, I can't be upset with my sister.

A second later, my phone vibrates again.

Jenna: I'm so sorry! Mom was frantic to know where you were and Izzy's lake house wasn't cutting it as an excuse because she ran into Izzy's mom.

Dammit.

A rush of tears burns the back of my eyes, but I don't let them fall.

I take a deep breath to calm my racing heart. Even though last night was a mistake—I married a man whose last name I don't even fucking know in Vegas—I don't regret anything about the time I spent, and the way I felt, with Leif. For that alone, I'm grateful. Because he reminded me that I can feel alive and cherished and *enough* again.

Mom continues to message and that's my cue.

I slip from the bed, clean up, locate my clothes, and dress.

I ignore Mom's messages and text Izzy instead.

Then, I spend a long moment staring at the beautiful man

who made love to me last night. He will never know that he healed a piece of the broken inside me. For the first time in years, I truly felt like myself with a man. Not scared or doubtful, but free and confident. Bending over his frame, listening to his gentle snore, I smile and press a kiss to his temple. "Thank you, Leif."

While I'm thanking him for the night we shared, I doubt he'll see it that way when we need to sort out the annulment papers. But right now, I need to leave.

Slip away before he wakes up and acknowledges the crushing disappointment of marrying me last night.

I swipe up my heels, pad barefoot to the hotel door, let out an exhale, and leave Leif behind.

Then, I slide my purple ring off my finger, tuck it into my purse, and do the walk of shame back to my hotel.

Another good thing about Vegas? No one gives a shit.

After a hot shower and a quick breakfast with the girls, we're boarding a flight back to Minnesota.

I have three messages and two phone calls from Tennessee, but I ignore them. I'm not sure what we're supposed to do next. I'm out of my comfort zone and need to reserve my energy to face off with Mom and move to Knoxville. Plus, I'm not ready to confront a sober, awake, and disappointed Leif.

So, I turn off my phone, plop down in my seat, and force myself to fall asleep before take-off.

SIX

Leif

Tennessee: Knoxville, what gives?

Tennessee: You know that's how you're saved in my phone.

Tennessee: Even though you're my wife. Legally, I mean.

Tennessee: Come on, you're seriously gonna ghost me, Cam?

I toss my phone down and grip the back of my neck.

"Dude, I can't believe you beat me to the fucking altar," Chris cackles.

"Me too." Hudson raises his hand, but his expression is more serious than the rest of the guys.

I squeeze the back of my neck, as if the pressure there

will alleviate the pounding in my head. Cami straight up bounced on me.

I turn away from my friends in the swanky hotel suite and pour another cup of coffee from the room service someone ordered this morning. Just keep the caffeine coming.

"Aw, come on, y'all at least had a wedding night, didn't you?" Fucking Ray thrusts his hips.

"If you're doing it like that, it's no wonder you're not getting action," Chris snorts.

I burn the roof of my mouth and bite back my swear.

"Give Leif a break," Hudson chides the guys.

"My wife fucking ghosted me," I spell it out for my friends. "You guys, I legally married Cami."

"Damn," James mutters. "Annulment can be a bitch."

"Screw that. Divorce is gonna be a bitch," Ray adds. "You're a fucking professional hockey player."

"You think she knew?" Chris wonders.

I shake my head. "No, I don't. And honestly? I don't think she would care one way or the other."

"Until you see her in court," James mutters.

"Fuck." I scrub a hand down my face. Even though annulment and divorce are the obvious outs to my current dilemma, both options sour my stomach. For a handful of hours last night, wrapped up in Cami, I felt...home. It doesn't make any damn sense, but I still can't believe she dipped out on me this morning.

Unless she regrets it. My stomach twists at the thought.

No regrets, she said. But she said that while tipsy and in the moment. Things look different in the daylight.

Frustration builds in my body, and I take another swig of my coffee.

"Pool party?" Ray offers.

Hudson slings an arm around my neck and squeezes. "Come on. A piña colada will cheer you up."

"Jesus," I mutter, shoving him off me. "I married a fucking stranger and—"

"She did the walk of shame to not have to face you in the morning," James calls me out.

"Yeah," Ray agrees thoughtfully. "She definitely doesn't know you're a hockey player." His expression brightens. "That could be good, bro. Less attention."

"I'll make sure the bartender adds an umbrella to your beverage," Chris promises, throwing a pair of swim trunks at me.

"Come on. It's our last day in Vegas. Tomorrow, it's back to reality." Ray cuts me a look. "And for some of us, reality is going to suck."

I snort and shake off their ribbing. I head to my bedroom, ignore the indent of Cami on the left side of the bed, and change. Glancing around the space, there's no trace that she was even here save for the rumpled bedsheets. She really did slip away with the morning light and like a goddamn chump, I want to chase after her.

Hell, my brothers would never believe it if they could see me now.

I don't stress shit like this. I'm cool. Laid-back. Easygoing.

Jensen's last text message flickers through my mind.

Jensen: How crazy? You good?

I heave out a sigh. I'm definitely not good.

She gave me fucking stakes. And then, she bailed.

My chest feels tight, a pang slashing across my pecs. I press my palm to the center of my chest, as if it will help ease the pressure gathering there.

I want something—*someone*—to care about. I want more than...*this*. The piña colada and the easy pussy.

But I'm an idiot for thinking it could be my *wife*. Hell, Cami is just a stranger who I met in Vegas.

I work a swallow but all I taste is sour disappointment.

Still, I wanted it to be her.

Dragging my palms over the weed leaves imprinted on my bathing suit, I decide the only thing left to do is enjoy the day. Cami is ignoring my messages and right now, I can't handle the thought of her regretting us getting married. Besides, if she wants to pretend this shit never happened, that's her prerogative. Eventually, it will catch up to her.

But not today.

Today, I'm going to chill poolside with my buddies, drink a fucking piña colada, and try to forget the beautiful woman who flipped my world upside down.

"I want a straw too!" I holler as I reenter the communal space.

A cheer goes up from my friends.

"There he is! Laid-back Leif." Ray whips a bottle of sunscreen at my head.

I catch it and slip it into my backpack.

"Lead me to the pool," I demand as Chris laughs.

Then, I follow my friends and allow myself to roll with it. I proceed to get shitfaced. And sunburned.

And yeah, a little fucking heartbroken too. But no one else needs to know that.

BY THE TIME I'm back in Knoxville, I'm hopped up on frustration and anger—two emotions I dislike. I pride myself on taking things in stride, but when Cami offered me stakes, and I said I wanted them, I didn't realize how much that decision would affect my outlook.

Knowing I've got a wife running around who won't reply to a damn text message is infuriating. And hurtful.

I'm out of my element.

Needing to blow off steam, I head to the gym. The arena where the Thunderbolts play, the Honeycomb, is pretty quiet in the summer months. The players who have family out of town have headed home or have booked a vacation out of Knoxville.

It's a relief, since the last thing I need is to be hounded with questions by my teammates. I was traded in the middle of last season, right before the Christmas trading freeze, and while I've got a good rapport with my teammates, I'm still relatively new.

Jensen calls as I'm tossing my bag in the locker room.

I pick up. "What's good?"

"I'm ready to ask you that. You never replied to my text," he says.

I sigh, not ready to go into details, so I give him a version of the truth. "Just a wild night. I got a matching tattoo with a woman I hooked up with." But my stomach sours when I think of Cami as only a hookup. She's so much more than that it's not even funny.

"Damn, Leif." Jensen chuckles. "I hope it's not her name."

"Nah." I inject lightness into my tone and glance at the curling wave on my wrist. "Got a wave."

"Another fucking wave." I can hear my brother rolling his eyes.

"Yeah. But listen, I just got to the gym."

"Okay, I'll let you go. One thing—you talk to Mom?"

"Today? No, why?" I pause, my curiosity rising.

Jensen sighs. "Could be nothing but I haven't heard from her. King couldn't get in touch with her either."

Unease sweeps my veins. "You think—"

"She could be coming to see you, Leif." Jensen chuckles as my nausea increases.

"No way," I spit back. "She'd at least call."

His laughter grows. "I don't know, little brother. But if Mom shows up on your doorstep, run."

I snort. "She's not that bad."

"She's on a mission, Leif. Be prepared," he warns.

Since the start of last season, Mom has successfully ensured that King, Jake, and Jensen are matched up with the right women. But little does she—or anyone else know—I'm now a married man.

"Don't worry about Mom," I say, wanting to reassure him. And myself.

Jensen laughs again. "I'm not. That's for you to worry about now. Have a good workout."

"Talk soon," I reply, ending the call.

I sigh heavily and stow my phone. The last thing I need is Mom showing up in Knoxville. But right now, I'm at the gym to clear my head.

When I step into the gym, the clanking of weights causes me to pause. I don't want to deal with anyone right now—even less after Jensen's phone call. But, when I note it's our team captain, Damien Barnes, I relax and venture into the space.

"Hey!" He sits up on a bench and drags a towel across his face. "What's up, Leif?"

I shrug and move toward a rack of dumbbells. "Same old. How are you doing?"

Barnes studies me for a beat. He's quiet and thoughtful. More introspective and polished instead of the usual rough-around-the-edges, rowdy athlete. He's also locked down with a serious girlfriend—ahem, fiancée—Harper who is a fun-loving, chill woman I hit it off with immediately.

At least my team captain is cool and the furthest thing from a gossip.

"Not bad. Harper's in Aspen this week, visiting my sister." He takes a swig from his water bottle.

"You didn't want to visit your sister, too?" Given that we now have some off time, I'm surprised Barnes held back.

He snorts. "I know. I'd usually tag along but Fiona, that's my sister, recently got engaged. Her fiancé took my nephew Garrett on a fishing trip, and Fi and Harper are dress shopping. With my mom. Definitely steering clear of that."

"Oh. That sounds nice," I comment.

Barnes snickers. "You don't know my mom."

The corner of my mouth tugs up on its own accord. I think about the past year and how meddlesome my mom's been in setting up my brothers. She would love an opportunity to dress shop for any wedding.

Silver lining—at least I'm technically married and there-fore, as soon as Mom hears of this news, I'm no longer a target. I just hope I can tell her before she appears like Jensen insinuated.

I tell Barnes, "Trust me, Mama Bang could probably give her—and any other mom—a run for her money." I lift an eyebrow. "Six kids—including five boys who play in the NHL. My mom takes no prisoners."

Barnes chuckles. "Fair. You may actually have me beat with that. So, how was Vegas?"

I hesitate, wondering how much I should share. Barnes is my team captain and, as far as I've seen, a strong leader and a discreet teammate. I sigh. "How much time do you have?"

He freezes and looks me over. "How badly do you need a workout?"

I shake my head. "Just blowing off steam."

"Would a beer suffice?"

I nod. "Corks?"

"Let's go grab a brew and a bite," he agrees, standing from the bench.

Even though I still feel restless energy coursing though my limbs, I know sitting down with Damien and talking shit through will be its own kind of therapy. Right now, I could use the sounding board. Maybe even his advice.

We head into the locker room, and I change back into my shorts and a T-shirt while Barnes takes a quick shower. When we're both dressed, we head to Corks. I park behind him, we enter the popular sports bar, and we snag a table in the back.

Around us, televisions broadcasting the summer Olympic Games show highlights from a recent basketball game and swim competition. We place our orders and make small talk.

But after the first sip of beer, Damien cuts to the chase. "Vegas?"

I shake my head slowly, rolling the cold bottle of beer between my hands.

Damien swears softly. "How much did you lose?"

I look up. "It's not that."

He frowns. "Not gambling? Then, what?"

"I got married." I practically announce it and the server approaching our table with a board of nachos gasps in surprise.

Damien drops his head and the server places down the board and scurries away.

"Okay," my team captain breathes out, remaining his cool, calm demeanor. We share that trait. "Okay." His eyes flick up to meet mine. "What is she hitting you with? Money? A lawsuit? A scandal? Pictures? Just, lay it out for me, man."

"Nothing," I admit.

Damien stares at me like I'm an alien. "What do you mean, nothing?"

"She ghosted me, bro." I snort and grip the back of my neck. "Fuck, I don't know why it's bugging me this much. I barely know the woman and yet—she's straight up ghosting me, and I can't fucking stand it."

"Hold up." Barnes lifts a hand. "Do you, Leif, do you like this woman?"

"I think so," I admit, surprising the hell out of both of us. "But right now, I just need her to talk to me. And she's—"

The shrill ring of my phone cuts me off.

I pull my cell from my pocket and glance at the screening, frowning when I read Mom's name. No fucking way.

"Give me a second," I tell Barnes. "It's my mom."

He leans back in his chair and lifts his beer.

"Mom," I answer, about to tell her it isn't a good time to talk.

"Leif, how many times do I have to tell you that a fake rock is an awful place to hide a key? I found it in about three seconds. If I can spot it, anyone can," Mom rambles through the line.

I straighten in my chair trying to play catch up. "Mom, what do you mean? Where are you?"

Mom exhales but the sound is...cheery. "I'm here, Leif! And I must tell you, you've done an excellent job with the aesthetic of your place. It could use some tidying but, well, that's another reason why I'm here, right? Say, when will you be home?" she continues in a singsong voice, as though this is normal.

As though I should have expected her to show up in

Knoxville. And, given Jensen's phone call an hour ago, I should have.

A conversation from weeks ago with my brother Jensen flickers through my mind.

If Mom shows up on your doorstep, run.

Oh, fuck.

I groan.

Across from me, Damien gives me a look.

"I'm just grabbing a bite with my team captain," I tell my mother. "I'll be home in a bit. Do you need anything?"

"Oh, no! Don't worry about me. I'll make myself at home and see you soon!" She hangs up.

I drop my cell phone to the tabletop.

"What's going on?" Barnes asks. "Did your family find out? Is your mom—"

"Here," I interject. "My mom is here. In Knoxville. At my house. For a surprise visit or an... I don't know, an ambush."

Across the table, Barnes's eyes widen. "Shit, Leif. I think you were right. Mama Bang fucking wins."

Yeah. Mama Bang always wins.

SEVEN

Cami

"This is the last bag," I tell Mom as I carry a massive shopping bag in from the trunk of my new car. Well, a used car—it's a used, white Honda Civic—but it's new to me. Dad and Rhett talked at length about the best car I can buy within my budget and when the Civic—or Civiche as I've taken to calling her—became available, they negotiated a fair price. All Mom and I had to do was pick her up after we landed in Knoxville three days ago.

Since then, we met the landlord of the apartment I rented, gave it a deep clean, and have been shopping for home goods and decor. Now, we're nearing the finish line and I must admit, my apartment has come together beautifully. Simple, but lovely.

My phone buzzes in my pocket and I glance at the screen.

> Tennessee: How long are you going to avoid me?

> Tennessee: We at least need to talk, Cam. Didn't take you for a coward.

Ouch! That stings but...it's a fair accusation. My palms break out in a sweat, and I drag them over my cut-off shorts. The thick watch strap I've been wearing to cover up my new ink catches on the pocket of my shorts. It's been a constant reminder of that night with Leif.

I've been ignoring him and his messages for the past week, since I left Vegas and tried to unsuccessfully push my graduation celebration—my fucking wedding—from my mind.

It's too reminiscent of the time I spent with Levi. And yet, it's entirely different.

The conversation Leif and I had walking around Vegas was meaningful. There was a depth I never shared with Levi and that alone scares me. I don't know if I can trust it.

Am I being naïve? Am I being carefree and impetuous Cami?

Or can I lean into my attraction for Leif and explore it further? Sure, marrying him was a mistake but I can't deny enjoying the time we spent together.

I sigh. Either way, he's right. I can't avoid him forever.

I also don't want to confront him with Mom here. That will make everything infinitely worse. No, when I speak with Leif, it needs to be just the two of us.

I can't deal with Mom's hysterics as she relives the nightmare that followed my time in Spain. The naked photos Levi took of me with drugs in the background. The toxicology reports that confirmed I had drugs in my system. The lawyers that needed to be hired to obtain the photos that could ruin my life before it even began.

The advice she doled out and I ignored. Again.

Take your time. Use your head. Be cautious.

Marriage in the middle of the night to a stranger in Vegas is the opposite of all her advice combined.

"Are you sure you want a green couch?" Mom asks for the third time, wrinkling her nose.

I slip my phone back into my pocket and sigh.

I should clarify—my apartment is lovely to me. "Mom, it's sage. It's soft and calming and—yes, I like it."

"Well, it's your apartment," she agrees in defeat.

I hold back my comment. As much as I appreciate Mom's help, three days locked in an apartment with her is starting to grate on my nerves. It's the commentary that scrapes at me.

I dig through the final shopping bag and pull out towels and linens that I drop right into the washing machine. Then, I stand in the center of the small living room and spin.

The apartment has stark white walls but with a cream rug, light oak furniture I scored from Ikea, the sage green couch I thrifted, and framed photos on the walls that Mom and I had to watch a YouTube tutorial to hang, I love it. "It's perfect."

Mom sighs again but this time it's less judgy. She wraps an arm around my waist, and I drop my head to her shoulder.

"We did it," I tell her.

She gives me a little squeeze. "We sure did. I'm proud of you, Cami."

I turn to look at her.

She gives me a small smile. "This job, this apartment, your move... It's good for you. You'll have more of a routine, a consistency—stability."

I bite my bottom lip and nod. This is exactly what Mom

wants for me. Even though she doesn't say it, I know she thinks that once I'm settled down, she can relax and stop worrying.

Rhett and Jenna never gave her and Dad the hard times I did. While they move in linear lines, I've been zigzagging since day one.

Underage drinking in high school. Doing whatever Levi Rousell asked of me and believing everything he told me in the weeks before he entered rehab. Having to deal with the constant panic of those photos leaking on the internet.

For seeking out freedoms—little things like snow-tubing with my girlfriends at three AM and sleeping in late—that Mom likes to criticize and make me feel guilty for.

I don't think she means to pick at my life as much as she harbors guilt for my mistakes with Levi. She doesn't want a repeat occurrence. Her insistence on stability and routine, on accounting and safe jobs, has been her mantra for the past three years. Hell, for the entirety of my college career.

And I've tried to live up to it. I've tried to make her proud, even at the expense of myself.

I can't deny Mom the peace of mind she's after, but I'm also tired of tamping down my own hopes and desires.

Still, I give her the words she needs to hear. "Yeah. It will be good for me."

Mom smiles brightly and glances at her watch. Surprise rolls over her expression. "Oh! It's already three PM."

"Okay." I frown. Are we on a schedule I don't know about?

Mom places a hand on her stomach. "We missed lunch."

Man, her routine is stressful.

"Let's go into the downtown and have a bite," she says brightly. She smiles and for a moment, she looks like the mother from my adolescence. A lot calmer and more carefree.

"We should celebrate—you're all moved in." She gestures around the space.

"Okay," I laugh, moving to the front door to grab my sneakers.

"Oh, don't you think you should shower first?" Mom asks. "We're all sweaty and ugh, we should freshen up."

I roll my eyes but nod. "I'll rinse off quickly."

Mom grins. "Great! I'll take the guest bathroom. I think we should aim for four PM, okay?"

What is going on? "Okay."

Mom grips the handle of her small suitcase and rolls it right into the bathroom.

My stomach grumbles as my phone buzzes again.

> Tennessee: Cam, we need to have a conversation. We need to figure things out.

I groan. He's right; I know he is. But, instead of replying, I do as Mom expects and enter the master bathroom. I flip on the showerhead, go through the motions, and freshen up for lunch.

Tomorrow, Mom flies home. Tomorrow, I'll talk to Leif.

"DID I tell you I have a friend in Knoxville?" Mom asks as we walk toward a restaurant she looked up and wants to try.

"Seriously?" I glance at her.

She smiles and links her arm with mine. "Yes! She's a friend from St. Paul but she's actually in town this weekend. Oh, we've been friends for years."

"Let me guess—she's meeting us for lunch?"

Mom flushes and dips her chin, confirming my hunch.

I snort. "Why didn't you say anything? I would love to

meet your friend." It's true too. I appreciate Mom coming to Knoxville with me to help me settle in. The least I can do is have lunch with her and a friend she wants to visit with.

"Really?" Mom's smile turns natural. "Good. I met her when I was pregnant with Rhett. She has six kids—"

"They must have the best Christmas mornings!"

Mom snorts. "I don't think I could have done it, but Stella is better at the juggling act than me. Much more laid-back and always had a better handle on things."

I give Mom's arm a squeeze. What happened with Levi is hardly her fault and yet, I know it eats at her. I think that's partly why I've gone along with her expectations and "suggestions" about how I live my life for as long as I have. I hate that she blames herself for my poor decisions.

"Why is she in Knoxville? Did she move here?" I ask.

"Oh, no. She's visiting her son."

I pause. "Mom." Don't tell me this is a setup. Worse—an ambush!

Mom widens her eyes and grins brightly. "It's just lunch, Cami."

"Ugh, come on," I groan. "You didn't even give me a heads-up."

"I want you to know someone in this new city. A contact, someone you can reach out to, in case of an emergency."

"I'm sure I'll make friends at work."

"I'm sure you will too. But would this really hurt? Stella's son is relatively new to town, too. He's a nice guy. A few years older than you. He travels for work so it's not like he's going to be a constant fixture in your life—just a friendly face to grab a Friday dinner with or call if you have car trouble."

"Fine," I agree, rolling my eyes.

I hate when Mom meddles like this. She hasn't intervened since her plan to set me up with her dentist's son failed. Sigh. At least with this dude, Mom will be back in Minnesota and if I never speak to him again, she won't be any wiser.

"We're here," Mom says, gesturing toward a cute restaurant. She reaches for the door handle and pulls it open.

We enter and I freeze.

Because sitting at a table with a broadly grinning and frantically arm-waving woman is Leif.

My husband.

And he looks devastatingly sexy and downright furious.

EIGHT

Leif

I freeze when I see her.

She looks beautiful. Surprised.

Fucking guilty.

"Leif." Mom gives my shoulder a nudge.

I stand from the table as Cami and her mother approach.

"I've known Cheryl for years," Mom reminds me, as if I'm eight and need more of an incentive to not embarrass her. Or myself.

But—out of all the women my mom has befriended in her life, she was planning to introduce me to...my wife?

I need a shot of tequila.

"Stella!" Cheryl beams, opening her arms to pull Mom into a hug.

Over their heads, I glare at Cami.

Her eyes are wide, her lips parted, and she looks like she's about to pass out. But I can't shake my anger. I tried to get in touch with her. I called, I texted, hell, I even searched for her on U of M's social media handles.

Which, after extensive hours of research, I've concluded she doesn't have. Tell me that's not a red flag? A recent graduate of U of M, in a sorority, with no socials?

I narrow my eyes and she swipes her tongue over her bottom lip, nervous.

"This is my son, Leif," Mom introduces me to Cheryl.

I smile warmly and embrace my mother-in-law. "It's great to meet you, Cheryl."

Cheryl introduces Stella to me and Mom. Mom hugs Stella in greeting and I follow.

I lean closer, letting her light floral perfume wash over me. Her hair smells like coconuts and her skin is warm where I press my thumb into her bare shoulder.

"Leif." My name on her lips is a whisper. A warning and a plea.

"Where's your ring?" I mutter, too low for our mothers to hear. I flash her the one she fashioned me out of little rubber bands. Yep, I haven't taken it off because even though she disappeared, I made vows.

When I accepted her proposal for marriage, I believed she was giving me *stakes*. I trusted that she saw me for me and understood things on a level no one else cared to see. And then, she fucking disappeared, and I haven't been able to chill out since.

So much for being laid-back. Cami gave me exactly what I asked for and yet, I didn't anticipate this version of it at all.

She stiffens at the question, and I pull away before our mothers pick up on the strange vibe between us.

The four of us sit down at the table.

I rub my hands together and quirk an eyebrow at Cami.

This just got interesting.

Our server comes by before the awkwardness has the opportunity to properly settle over our table. The server eyes me for a long moment, no doubt trying to place me, and I hide behind my menu before she can call me out. Now is not the time for Cami to learn I play hockey for the Thunderbolts.

Mom and Cheryl each order a glass of wine so I ask for a beer.

Cami—cool, confident, carefree Cami—looks like she wants to vomit. She's sitting on her hands and her shoulders are bunched around her ears.

If I was really meeting her for the first time, I'd think she was nervous around new people. But I know better. I've seen her in action, dancing in clubs. I held her hand when she got a tattoo. I've heard the sweet moans that fall from her lips when she comes.

Shit. I drop my eyes to the table as Cami says, "I'll take a margarita, thanks."

"A margarita?" Cheryl questions—like everyone else at the table didn't toss out an alcoholic beverage.

How else are we supposed to endure this lunch-turned-drinks-turned-shitshow?

"How are you settling in, Cami?" Mom interjects, smoothing things over the way she's apt to do. Either that or shaking everything upside down like a snow globe and watching where the pieces land.

I frown. Is this what she did to King and Jakob and Jensen? Oh, shit. Realization dawns as horror sweeps through me. I glare at my mother's profile.

She was setting me up with Cami—for real. Not just as a, "hey I'd appreciate it if you'd occasionally check in on my friend's kid since she just moved to town" way. But a, "I'm desperate for all my children to find love and settle down so

I'm going to orchestrate for you to fall in love with this stranger."

And then, that stranger is already my fucking wife.

I choke on my laughter and slap myself on the chest. Cami gives me a look.

Dammit, we'll have to tell them. The moms will need to know the truth so that Cami and I have a chance to work through this like adults without our mothers trying to play matchmaker behind the scenes.

I push away from the table abruptly and all eyes swing in my direction.

"Leif?" Mom questions. Her smile is tight. Ha! I guess I did need that silent, not so subtle, warning about not embarrassing her.

"Sorry." I clear my throat and point toward the bar. "I need a water and it looks like our server needs a hand."

"I'll, uh, I'll help," Cami volunteers, standing too.

Her mother gives her a look she ignores and the two of us relocate to the bar, making sure to round it so we're out of our mothers' lines of vision.

"What the hell is going on?" Cami hisses, some of her spunk returning.

It's such a relief to see that I don't call her on it. Besides, we don't have time. "Our mothers are setting us up."

"Well, yeah." She tosses a hand in the air. "I got that part. My mom's been doing this for the past few months, ever since —" she cuts herself off and shakes her head.

Ever since what? I want to ask but I don't.

Instead, I offer, "Yeah, my mom's been on a rampage as well. She's spent the last year bouncing between my brothers' places, setting them up and screwing with their lives."

Cami works a swallow. "Did it work?"

I consider her question. Think about King and Rory, Jake

and Gardenia, Jensen and Bailey. "I guess so. But I'm not like my brothers. And besides—"

"We're already married."

"That." I flag down a bartender. "Can we get two shots of tequila?"

"Tequila?" Cami looks horrified. She leans to the left and quickly straightens. "Our mothers are right there."

I shrug. "My mom will expect this from me."

"My mom..." Confusion crosses her expression.

"What?"

"My mom will too," she admits, disappointed.

My eyebrows tug together as I try to understand the dynamic between Cami and her mother. It's complicated, that's for sure.

I flip my chin at her wrist and the watch she's wearing. "She know about the tattoo?"

Cami snorts. "Not yet." She looks at me, her blue eyes turning softer. Honest. "I was ignoring you."

I snort. "No shit."

"I was scared," she admits, biting the corner of her mouth. "But, honestly, I was going to call you tomorrow after my mom left. It's..." She pauses to shake her head. "I can't do this with you with her...here."

"I get that, babe. I do." The tension between Cami and her mom is obvious to strangers. "But we gotta come clean."

Her eyes slam into mine and I watch terror swirl in her irises.

Damn. What the hell went down between her and her family? I reach for her hand and press my thumb into her wristband. A gentle reminder of the ink hiding beneath—a wave. Weren't we supposed to ride the wave of life?

Yes, I get how fucking corny it is. But we were drunk. Case in point—we hit up the chapel right afterwards.

"All you can do is crest and coast," I murmur, recalling words my grandfather, my dad's dad from Norway, told me when I was a little kid.

"What?" Cami asks.

The bartender places down our tequila shots and I toss some bills on the bar.

Taking my shot glass, I turn to her. "Getting married was your idea."

"I know," she hisses, her cheeks turning red. "It was a spur-of-the-moment thing."

I arch an eyebrow. "Proposing to me? I confessed a fucking secret—something no one knows about me—and you gave me the gift I was asking for and then bounced."

She closes her eyes and exhales. When she opens them, I note the regret rounding out her irises and it makes me feel worse.

"Don't you dare pity me," I snap.

Cami sighs. "I'm not. I'm...relating."

"To what?"

"To you." She throws a hand in my direction. "I didn't want you to wake up and be disappointed that you legally tied yourself to me."

"Why the hell would I be disappointed?" I bite out, my frustration swirling with my confusion. Right now, I don't feel calm or chill. I feel nervous and a little out of control.

Dammit.

"Because, Leif, I...I make mistakes."

"Everyone does! We're human." Wait a second. "I thought you didn't do regrets?"

"I don't regret marrying you," she admits, soothing my main concern. "But I don't know how to navigate this next part."

I shake my head and gesture toward the table our mothers

are seated at. "Neither do I. My mom is on a mission and it looks like yours is too." I hold up my hand when Cami starts to explain. "It doesn't matter what the reasons are. But if we have any chance of working this out"—I gesture between us—"then we need to come clean. Our moms will give us some space if they know the truth."

"That we know each other from Vegas?"

Oh, God. I shake my head. "That we're married," I remind her. My brothers and friends would die of laughter if they could see me now. Standing here, trying to convince this beautiful woman that a marriage with me is worth a shot.

"Wait..." She pauses to toss back her tequila shot. "I need another," she tells the bartender.

Snorting, I take my shot as well and smack my lips together. I shake my head when the bartender gestures at my glass. "I'm fine with one, thanks."

Cami rolls her eyes. "So, you want to...stay married?"

I shrug.

"Why?" She nearly vibrates with frustration. Confusion. Fear. "Why the hell wouldn't you want an annulment? We have a shot, you know. I looked into it."

"Oh, did you? Extensively, I bet with your move across the country and your vanishing act."

Cami laughs—surprising the hell out of me. The musical sound relaxes me some and I find myself grinning back.

"Fine. I barely looked at the requirements, but I thought you'd want to end this as quickly as possible."

"I'm not most guys, remember?" I say gently. "Cam, I admitted to you that I want stakes. That I want more. That deep down, I want the type of marriage, the type of family and home, that my parents built."

"I know," she murmurs.

"Yeah, I may be known as the chill, laid-back dude, but I

don't shirk my commitments. I've never been the type of guy who makes promises and breaks them. I made vows to you, Cami. I'm not okay with a divorce when we didn't even *try* to make it work." I pause, searching her face for any expression that will clue me in to her thoughts.

Even though it's insane that we married without knowing each other for more than a handful of hours, it felt right. Hell, when I confessed my secret, and she offered me a solution— offered me *her*—I thought she was granting me a gift.

"This is my first time on my own," she murmurs. "Truly on my own."

"Okay."

"I never had the chance to figure things out for myself and now..." she trails off, lifting her arm in my direction and letting it fall.

"I'd never hold you back from your dreams," I say softly. "I don't care if you're an accountant or not. I'd support you if you want to do drawing or a more creative profession."

Her eyes snap to mine and widen. She blinks, as if seeing me in a new light. "Leif," she whispers.

I shuffle forward half a step. "Cam, my mom is here, staying with me, to set me up and see me settled. Your mom obviously wanted you to meet me."

"My mom just wants me to have a traditional life," she clarifies.

"What's wrong with that?"

"It's not what I want!" She grips the second shot glass and tosses it back.

I grin. But isn't she hot when she's stressed? Unraveling in all the right ways. "What do you want, Cam?"

She freezes. Those blue eyes snap to mine and hold. "I want..." she sighs. "I want to start my life. On my own terms. Not as someone's wife. But as me, Cami Coleman."

I reach out to tuck a strand of hair behind her ear. Cami Coleman. I like her full name.

"I'm not in love with you, Leif," she continues.

"That's fair. I'm not in love with you either," I admit. What I don't say is I've never been this twisted up over—this affected by—a woman. "You don't know me. Yet." I tuck a hand in the pocket of my jeans. Shrug. "I'm very lovable."

She snorts. "What if we give this a fair shot and it... doesn't work?"

"Then, we get divorced," I agree. "But do you really want to dissolve everything without a fair chance? We're obviously attracted to each other." I brush my fingertips over her lips, and she nearly shudders. "Our families won't oppose it." I tilt my head toward our mothers who are probably wondering what the hell happened to us. "And we could at least see what this spark between us is. 'Cause there's something here, Cam. I've never done a serious relationship thing—my first attempt can't crash and burn."

She blinks and her eyes clear. She watches me for a long moment. Tilts back again to check on our mothers. "Fine." She pushes her hair behind her ears. "Fine, we'll...give this a chance."

I smile. "Good."

"Being with you will help get my mom off my back too," she adds. "She'll feel better about my move here and give me some space. This arrangement, while temporary, is...also a convenient distraction for my mom."

I can't fault her for her honesty...but I hope this "arrangement" becomes more than just a temporary convenience. "Another item for the pro column."

Cami nods and then her eyes swings to mine, wide and worried. "Ah, your mom is coming!"

I grin. God, isn't she great?

She shakes out her wrists and practically prances from one foot to the next. I chuckle and reach for her. Then, I pull her into my frame, drop my mouth to hers, and kiss her hard. I swallow her worries and prove that we can give this a real chance.

A promising start.

NINE

Cami

His mouth lands on mine like a balm to my wounds—the ones that are still healing, the ones that are just smarting.

When Leif kisses me, my mind clears. The stress melts away. The worries and doubts and fears subside. There's just me and him and this. The moment.

His tongue slips inside, and I angle my head, wanting to deepen our kiss. His hands slide to the top of my ass, his fingertips grazing the back pockets of my jeans. My hands are trapped against his chest, and I love that I can feel the beat of his heart through his shirt.

It's steady. Centering. Here.

"Leif Bang!" His mother's voice cuts through my head, and I jump back, dazed.

Gah! I knew she was coming and I—Leif's smirk cuts off my thought.

How does he do that? Why is he so distracting?

Leif Bang.

"Your last name is Bang?" I blurt out. "As in—"

"Don't finish that sentence," he interrupts, his eyes dancing.

Stella rolls her eyes. "Like I haven't heard that one before."

"I'm so sorry, Mrs. Bang," I stutter. Wince.

Leif laughs.

"Stella," I amend.

Stella grins. "Don't apologize, love. I know what a charmer Leif can be. I've been watching him get his way with the ladies for years now."

Leif gapes at his mother for calling him out. I blush from her meaning but can't help but laugh.

So I married a playboy.

Of course, I did. Leif is *exactly* my type. And yet, nothing like what I'm used to.

"I knew I knew you!" our server says, staring at Leif from the server station next to the bar. She's pointing at him. "You're a Bolts player! You got traded right before Christmas. Man, it was rough when y'all didn't make the playoffs but y'all are gonna have a great season. Losing Hardt to San Jose was tough and then Daire retired." She shakes her head. "But we're really happy you're here," she adds although I don't see this "we" she speaks of. And who the hell are these people?

My mind whirls. The Bolts...as in the Thunderbolts!

Realization dawns and I gawk at Leif.

"You're a hockey player!" I hiss.

He grins. "I am."

"I thought you were a surfer," I growl, shoving my bangs out of my eyes. I look at Leif but—I don't watch hockey. After Rhett stopped playing, my whole family kind of lost interest in the game. There's no way I would have placed him. Still, it seems like a huge thing not to disclose before saying "I do."

"I'm that too," he says defensively.

Stella watches us with wonder in her eyes. She doesn't look nearly as upset by our exchange as she should. Maybe because she doesn't know that the other shoe is about to drop.

"Come on, your mom is waiting. And getting worried," Stella continues, eyeing our empty shot glasses. "And clearly, there is a story that needs to be shared because you two"—she points between us—"*know* each other."

"Intimately," Leif mutters in response to the way his mother says *know*.

She doesn't hear him, but I do. I narrow my eyes at him.

His grin widens and he slips his hand in mine. Again, his thumb brushes over my watchband, reminding me of the tattoo hiding underneath. My drawing. A rolling wave. About to land on my fucking head and drown us all.

"You could've told me," I mutter.

"I could have," he agrees but doesn't offer an explanation as to why he wouldn't share his profession—as a freaking hockey player—with me.

My mother's pinched expression greets me as I plop down into the chair beside her. Oh no, can she smell the tequila on my breath?

"A shot?" she mutters.

Yep.

"My fault," Leif says smoothly, giving my mother an irresistible smile.

She softens and Stella arches an eyebrow at me as if to say—*see? He's charming.*

Oh, trust me, I know.

"So," Leif says slowly, "Cami and I are already acquainted."

"You are?" Mom leans forward.

"We are," Leif confirms, glancing at me.

I open my mouth, but words don't come out.

"Isn't that great?" Stella chimes in, saving me.

"Yes!" Mom gushes. "Now, you two can travel home to Minnesota together for holidays. Or grab a dinner every now and then. It will be easy for you to fall back into your friendship or—" She looks at Leif. "How do you two know each other?"

"It's actually a funny story," he starts, injecting enthusiasm into his warm tone. He doesn't look stressed out. Instead, he's as cool as a cucumber. He even leans back in his chair and takes a pull of his beer. His Adam's apple bobs and I try not to stare but... God, even his neck is hot.

Stop getting distracted! Your entire world is about to implode.

Except, it's not. Because that already happened and you're still here.

I take a deep breath to steady myself.

"Can't wait to hear it," Stella tacks on, her eyes dancing the same way her son's do. Like she's more amused than wary.

My mother looks positively frightened. So much so, her knuckles turn white from where she holds the stem of her wine glass. She clears her throat. Gives me a quick look. "If this has something to do with Cami's past—"

"It doesn't," I interject before she can give more away. Why did she have to mention my past mistakes at all? Not everyone knows about Levi! In fact, Mom, Dad, and their lawyers did such a great job that no one—save for my immediate family and a few close friends—knows anything at all.

Across the table, Leif's gaze snaps to mine. His nostrils

flare and his eyes narrow, as if trying to decipher Mom's words or my reaction. Probably both.

My toes begin to tap the floor. My knees bounce. I slip my hands under my thighs to stop their trembling. And then, I ramble. "It's silly, really. Just, a great night out. Our friend groups really hit it off and—"

"In Minnesota? Minneapolis?" Stella guesses.

"Vegas," I toss out.

"Vegas!" Mom exclaims. "You two, you know each other from Las Vegas?" She laughs nervously. "Well, you were just there, Cami. What a small world! How did you learn the connection?" She gestures between herself and Stella.

"We didn't," Leif says dryly.

"Oh!" Stella remarks, rolling her lips together as if to keep from laughing. "So, you two..." Her eyebrows waggle as she glances between us.

Mom turns positively red and takes a gulp of—nearly polishing off—her wine. "Camille," she squeaks.

"We hit it off right away," I toss out. "I mean, he's so charming, you know? You know, Stella."

Stella chuckles and nods.

Mom begins to fan herself.

"And I was taken with Cami's free-spirited outlook," Leif says and I know he means it as a compliment but Mom doesn't take it that way.

Her hand swats the air faster. "Oh, that's one way of describing her. Cami's a follower by nature."

Leif frowns. "Cami's one of the most fun women I've ever spent a night with." He drops his head as soon as his words color the air.

I groan.

Stella barks out a laugh and then hides it with a sip of her wine.

Leif flashes me an apologetic look.

Mom nearly has a coronary.

I start to sweat. It feels like everyone's eyes are on me and a flush works over my skin. I'd love to blame it on the tequila but I'm pretty sure it's just the knowledge that I have to come clean. Before Leif can add any more colorful descriptions of me.

"We got married!" I announce.

Leif's mouth drops open.

Stella freezes, looking shocked.

And Mom? Well, Mom drops her wine glass, and it shatters, little pieces of glass skittering over the tabletop. We all jump back as the white wine floods the table and drips to the floor.

"I'm so sorry!" Mom and I exclaim in unison.

For a heartbeat, I'm jarred back to an old memory.

To Levi. To the night he chucked a bottle of champagne off a balcony in Barcelona. He was wasted, high, and emotionally spiraling. I sighed with relief when it landed on the hood of a parked car instead of a passing person.

But when Levi advanced on me, his eyes wild and reckless, I was truly terrified for the first time in my life.

I drag my hand over my face at the memory, shielding my expression. That was the night everything went sideways. After that, Levi got on a plane, checked into rehab, and we never spoke again. Nope, all correspondence to gain access to the photos he took of me went through our lawyers. To this day, I'm still relieved they never leaked.

I drop my hand to find Leif staring at me with naked confusion and curiosity in his expression. He's managed to keep Mom and Stella in their seats and he's using all the napkins on the table to blot up the mess.

"I got it," the server says, appearing with a broom, dustbin, and towels. "This happens all the time."

"I doubt that," Leif manages with that half smirk.

I snort and roll my eyes, reaching for levity, as my heartbeat continues to pulse in my temples.

The server cleans our table efficiently. Once we're all seated again, she reappears with a tray of food.

A new type of tension hovers over the table as we stare at each other over the appetizers Mom and Stella must have ordered while Leif and I were kissing behind the bar.

"We're gonna need more alcohol," Leif suggests.

"Another round," Stella agrees.

The server offers a tight smile and nods, scurrying away.

"You got married," Mom repeats.

"It just happened," I offer.

Mom glares at me. "Camille Coleman, that doesn't just happen! What the hell were you thinking? After everything, *everything* that's happened." She looks at me with heartbreak in her eyes. "And now, you've got your whole future ahead of you. This job, this chance, and you—you get married to a stranger in Vegas!"

"He's not a stranger. You know him," I point out pathetically.

Mom groans, dropping her face into her hands. She pulls in a deep breath and for long moments, we all stare at her, waiting for her outburst. Except, it doesn't come. Instead, Mom lifts her head and the strangest expression crosses her face. "You're married, Cami."

I clear my throat. "I am."

"You're married to Leif," she repeats, her voice a bit dazed.

"Uh-huh," I agree.

Mom glances between us. "Married." She fixes me with

her gaze. "A divorce would be a travesty. A blemish to the reputation you worked so hard to restore."

"We're not getting divorced," Leif says seriously, pulling my mother's attention away from me. "I want to get to know Cami. I want to give our marriage a chance."

I let out a slow exhale.

"I want to make this work," Leif continues. His tone is sincere and if I'm not mistaken, his mother is looking at him with pride instead of disappointment.

Mom blinks slowly. The flush on her cheeks lessens and she relaxes in her chair. "You—you do?" She nods. "Good, that's good."

Oh, no. She doesn't think this is a terrible mistake. Instead, Mom believes I've finally chosen—albeit by accident—correctly. *A good boy from a good family.* She's going to back Leif and his crazy idea!

I look longingly at the bar, wishing I could dive behind it and polish off the entire selection of spirits.

Our server returns with fresh beverages.

"Thanks," I say, taking my Coke.

"From the bartender," she adds, placing down a shot of tequila.

I stifle a chuckle. Good man.

Mom grumbles her disappointment, but I grin and lift it in the bartender's direction in gratitude. I could use the liquid courage.

The bartender winks in response.

Leif looks less pleased, but he doesn't say anything. He's too busy glaring at the bartender who ignores his pointed stare.

Stella holds up a glass and gives me a soft, understanding smile. "Well, I guess congratulations are in order."

My nerves scatter, ricocheting around my body as I gulp for oxygen.

Mom laughs—the sounds surprised. Relieved.

Leif holds up his glass and Mom does the same.

"I wish you both a lifetime of happiness. Of love and joy. I wish you a big love, like the one I've shared with Lars," Stella says truthfully.

Leif looks thoughtful as he stares at his mom. My mom blinks rapidly, as if holding back tears. "And I wish you the same. This may not be a traditional love story, but marriage is a beautiful bond, a lifetime commitment."

In Vegas, I felt like my marriage to Leif was the start of an adventure. But right now, with Mom beaming at me, her expression stamped with acceptance, it feels restrictive.

A prison sentence. The words pop into my head, and my heart rate ticks up.

When we clink glasses, Leif eyes me with the same serious, solemn expression. It causes my stomach to twist because...we don't know each other. Until a few minutes ago, I didn't even know what he did for a living!

We don't know the first thing about marriage.

Hell, I'm a terrible example of what half of a romantic relationship should look like. I've never been in a healthy, committed, long-term relationship.

And I don't want my first experience to be as a married woman!

"You're really married?" Mom asks, as if she can't believe the turn of events. "You're really settling down with Leif?"

He flashes Mom his Rainbow Looms ring. I sigh heavily and dig the purple crown ring out my purse. I hold it up for her to see before I slide it onto my finger.

"Oh my goodness," she laughs, covering her mouth. But

she looks content. Joyful. Her expression softens. "It will be good for you to settle down properly, Cami," she whispers.

"And we can upgrade your ring," Leif promises.

"I like this one," I admit quietly, wishing we were still caught up in the euphoria of that night. Of those moments.

Before Leif declared he wanted to give our marriage a chance and Mom endorsed the ludicrous idea.

Stella smiles. Leif snorts.

And I toss back the shot of tequila.

TEN

Leif

"This entire lunch has been an emotional roller coaster," Cami admits, brushing her bangs out of her eyes as we stand in front of the cute bistro Mom found for lunch. Lunch that has turned into a hell of a lot more.

"It's been something," I agree, trying to get a read on this woman I should know deeply but can't read at all. "You gonna answer my calls now?"

She ducks her head sheepishly. "We need to talk."

"We need to date," I counter.

She bites her bottom lip. "Leif, I don't know how to be married."

"You don't have to." I touch her wrist. "I don't either. We just have to be honest. We just have to try."

I'm relieved she's willing to give this a chance. And as messed up as it is, I'm also relieved her mother backed me on it. While Cami may not want this marriage for the same reasons I do, with time, she'll see it was worth sticking around for. She can say it's convenient or temporary but for me, it's a chance to prove that what we have is real. There's something about her that draws me in and I'm not willing to give up without exploring it further. Besides, I've never truly failed at anything in my life because I've always kept at it until I improved. This will be no different.

Cami and I will settle into our relationship—our marriage—and we'll be better for it.

"I'll call you tomorrow, after Mom leaves," she promises.

"Okay, Knox," I agree, tugging on the end of her hair.

"Knox?"

"Short for Knoxville."

She snorts. "Better than babydoll, or cutie pie, or shmoopie."

"Shmoopie?" I laugh.

She rolls her eyes. "Oh, the stories I can tell you, Leif."

"I'm game when you are, babydoll."

Cami bites the corner of her lip. "It's just a story Izzy shared when she went on this date from hell."

"Do your friends know we got married?" I ask, recalling the girls she was in Vegas with.

She averts her gaze and shakes her head. "I didn't want to make this a thing." She gestures between us, meeting my eyes. "I didn't think it would last."

"But we're trying now," I remind her.

"Yeah." She glances at her mom through the front window of the cafe. Our mothers are chatting with a local baker they started a conversation with—probably trying to convince her to make us a wedding cake. "I guess we are."

I sigh. "Okay, well enjoy the rest of your time with Cheryl and we'll talk tomorrow."

She snorts. "Have you met my mom? The rest of tonight will not be enjoyable."

I give Cami a look. "More stories there?"

"A lot more," she admits. "Mom and I have a complicated relationship."

I dip my head in understanding. We all have our family dynamics. With four brothers and a sister, I've got my fair share too.

"And now," Cami sighs, "she's going to want to talk about wedding planning and floral arrangements. She's going to wonder where we'll live and if we want to buy a dog." She arches an eyebrow at me. "We can still get out of this—before the crazy begins."

My stomach twists at the suggestion. I know it's a valid point but the thought of losing her, of letting this thing between us go before giving it a true chance at success, bothers me. I tug on the edge of her hair. "Where's your sense of adventure, Camille?"

She smiles but it doesn't reach her eyes. "Don't say I didn't give you an out, Leif."

"I don't want one." I mean it, too.

Our moms come out of the restaurant, their arms linked, their heads bent together. I hold open my arms and Cami falls into them. I give her a hard hug. "We got this, Cam."

"Yeah," she murmurs, sounding less convinced than me. That's okay, I'll prove to her that we can make this work. That it will be for the best.

When Cami hugs Mom, I turn toward Cheryl.

"I know this is a huge surprise." I gesture toward the restaurant where it all when down.

Cheryl smiles. "I just want Cami happy, with a good, strong man."

"I want the best for your daughter," I agree.

"Good." She smiles, giving me a hug. "With a little direction, Camille will make a wonderful wife."

Something about her words strikes me as odd. I don't want Cami because I want a *wife*. I just want *her*.

Cheryl pulls back. "Thank you, Leif. Honestly, I feel so much better leaving Cami in Knoxville now that I know she has you. Her husband." She grins broadly. "And now, we can begin wedding planning!"

Mom laughs at Cheryl's enthusiasm, but Cami remains distant, quiet.

"See you later, Cam," I tell my wife, turning toward my little bungalow with Mom.

Cami waves and sets off in the opposite direction with her mother.

"Well..." I say, waiting for my mom to fill in the blanks.

She pinches the side of my ribs and twists the skin.

"Ouch!" I swat her hand away. "What the hell was that for?"

"You got married in Vegas and didn't tell me!"

"I wanted to talk to her first." I gesture down the street where Cami's back recedes. "She's been ignoring me."

Mom harrumphs. "Serves you right."

"You're the first to know in our family," I appease her.

She eyes me suspiciously. "Even before Jensen?"

"Yep," I confirm.

"And Annie?"

"Uh-huh."

Mom brightens slightly before sighing. "This is serious, Leif."

"I know, I know." I gesture with my hand to keep her calm.

She swats it away and then grabs it, linking our fingers together. "Marriage is a real commitment, Leif. I know you like to take things in stride, but this isn't like almost getting expelled from university or pranking the juniors hockey team or—"

"I know, Mom," I cut her off because I understand the point she is trying to make. "Things obviously escalated but I'm not treating Cami like a joke gone awry. I want to...I want to make things work with her." I work a swallow. "One day, I want what you and Dad have. Well, I don't want to be as serious as Dad."

Mom snorts but nods for me to continue.

"But I want that type of connection. One where you can have an entire conversation without saying a word. I want that level of trust, that admiration, the love that you and Dad share. I know a lot of people would say this is the wrong way to go about it but...is it? There's something about Cami I like."

"It's hardly conventional," Mom murmurs. "But then again, you never were one for the traditional."

I shrug. She squeezes my hand.

"Her mom..." Mom pauses, sorting out her thoughts. "Cheryl wants the traditional, the proper order of things for Cami."

"I caught that," I say. "I'm kind of surprised you and Cheryl are friends."

"Why would you say that?"

"I don't know." I shake my head. "Diane was so full of life. She was always laughing and joking and up for an adventure—well, she was a lot like you," I explain, referring to Mom's best friend who passed away. When she died, Mom lost a bit of her sparkle and I think her tour of her children's lives has been an attempt to reclaim some of it back. "Cheryl, she doesn't seem to have that same...spunk. Zest for adventure and excitement. Cami has it but I don't think she inherited it from Cheryl. Cheryl seems more serious and wanting

Cami to settle down more than wanting her to find the right fit."

"Good thing you think you're the right fit," Mom mutters. Then, she sighs. "Cheryl was...different years ago. I don't know all the ins and outs but with each of her children's arrivals into the world, the more serious, the more guarded, she became. I do know that something transpired while Cami was in college that changed Cheryl. Made her less willing to throw caution to the wind, so to speak. She wants her kids to follow a certain path, a more traditional trajectory."

"Something transpired that involved Cami?" I ask, glancing at Mom.

Mom rolls her lips together and my concern kicks up. How fucked up is it that Mom knows more about my wife than I do?

"Mom," I press for information.

Mom sighs. "I think so, Leif. But I don't know exactly what. Now that you're married, I'm sure you can glean the ins and outs on your own. In time."

"I hope so," I say, already knowing it won't be easy. Cami is spontaneous and fun to be with, but it seems like she holds her personal thoughts close to her chest. Kind of like me.

Mom nods. "Camille is going to hear an earful from Cheryl tonight. Cheryl is going to launch into wedding planning and dress shopping. She's going to want Cami to start a registry and probably even mention having children. I didn't want to add any more opinions to the conversation by voicing my worries."

"It's very unlike you to hold back."

Mom chuckles. "I know, but Cami seemed overwhelmed."

"She was," I agree. "What are they? Your worries?"

Mom stops walking as we near my house. She drops my

hand and turns to look at me. "I love you, Leif. I've always enjoyed your sense of adventure, your humor, your way of looking at the world. But this, marriage, is bigger than just you. It involves Camille and her life and her family. Of course, I will support you. And yes, it makes it easier to process because I know Cheryl. But this isn't one of those things that's going to be easy just because you've decided to master it. This involves another soul—someone else's personality and dreams and desires—and you have no control over that."

I suck in an inhale as Mom levels me with a look and a heaping of wisdom.

"It's a balancing act. A give and take. A compromise. Across the board. And it always changes," Mom advises. "If you're serious about Cami—and let's be honest here, you've never had a serious girlfriend—it's going to require you to grow in ways you've yet to tap into. If you want to keep her, make this marriage work, you're going to have to tap into that emotional intelligence fast. I want the best for you. I want to see you happy. But I also don't want you to try to make a marriage work because not doing so would mean divorce."

I flinch at the word and Mom catches it.

She offers a soft smile. "I don't agree with Cheryl's outlook on divorce. It's not a failure. Or a judgment. A lot of people work super hard at marriages that don't last because they're not the right fit. Not because they've failed or let themselves down."

"Maybe I'm more traditional than you thought," I toss out because I don't want to dig too deeply into Mom's words. Not after the events that transpired today.

Mom shakes her head. "You're stubborn." She pats my cheek. "If you want to talk about anything, I'm here." Her grin widens. "And I'll be here for the foreseeable future so at least if you need advice on wooing a woman, you got one ready to weigh in." She gives me a little wave and ends our conversation by turning to walk up my driveway.

"I don't need help wooing a woman!"

Mom's laughter floats behind her.

Rolling my eyes, I follow my mom into my home.

Although I'm secretly relieved Mom didn't lay into me— she probably knows it's a lost cause since I've always played a bit by my own rules—I still can't sleep.

At three AM, I text Cami.

> Me: Hey, Knox, how'd it all go down with your mom?

She surprises me by replying a few minutes later.

> Knoxville: Can't sleep, Ten?

I smirk at her abbreviation for Tennessee.

> Me: Nope. You?

> Knoxville: Not at all. We had a family meeting via Zoom.

I frown and sit up in bed, propping another pillow behind my back.

> Me: You okay? How'd it go?

> Knoxville: The fact that my dad and brother aren't on a flight here is a blessing. Dad thinks I should come back to MN. My sister Jenna was the only balanced voice of reason. Mom wants me to move in with you and has already ordered Thunderbolts gear.

I laugh at the bit about Cheryl ordering gear. Doesn't she know I'm going to outfit the entire Coleman clan with Thunderbolts swag?

But damn. Her dad wants her to come home. Her brother wants to board a flight. I grip my phone, my thumb hovering over the keypad. I don't know what to type because...my family has always had my back. Even when I mess up. Or don't fully appreciate the gravity of any given situation. I've never had to weigh in on a woman's life—her relationship with her family—before. I've never cared to.

I swear and fist the duvet with my other hand.

> Me: What do you think? Are you staying here?

I watch as the text bubbles appear and disappear several times before Cami replies.

> Knoxville: Yeah. I talked to Izzy, too. She helped me gain some perspective.

> Knoxville: Plus, I start my new job on Monday. I'm staying.

Relief fills my chest and I exhale loudly.

> Me: What perspective?

I'm curious for more. With Cami, I want to know everything she's thinking. I want to understand her.

> Knoxville: Just that there's no harm in trying.

I sigh. I was definitely hoping for more.

> Me: Let me take you to dinner tonight? 8 PM?

Again, those text bubbles dance.

> Knoxville: Okay.

> Me: We'll figure this out, Knox.

> Knoxville: We could just get divorced, Ten.

I bite the corner of my mouth. Obviously, if she straight up tells me she wants divorce papers, I'm not going to fight her on it but...

> Me: Truth time. Deep down, is that what you really want?

She doesn't reply for a long time even though I see she read my message. Fifteen minutes goes by and I'm about to toss my phone and try to get some sleep when it shakes in my palm.

> Knoxville: Pick me up at 8 PM.

> Knoxville: Pin to location.

I smile at her response. There's still...something between us.

> Me: Get some sleep, Knox. I'll see you soon.

> Knoxville: Night, Ten.

ELEVEN

Cami

"It's just dinner," I remind myself as I pace my small apartment waiting for Leif to pick me up. *Dinner with your husband.*

Ugh, I can't believe I'm married. I can't believe Mom thinks it's the best thing since sliced bread either.

My phone buzzes in my hand and I pause, closing my eyes.

Is it Leif canceling?

Disappointment fills me at the thought, and I let out a sigh of relief. Clearly, I want to go out with Leif tonight. I may not be keen about the marriage part but on some level, I am attracted to Leif and want to explore what's between us.

See, you can trust yourself. Leif isn't Levi. He's not manipulating you. He's just taking you to dinner.

I glance at my phone.

Izzy: It's nearly date time! YAY! Have fun.
HAVE HOT SEX. Call me and tell me
everything.

I snort at her message and shake my head. Before I can reply, my sister texts.

Jenna: Mom landed in MN. I'm going home
for the weekend.

Me: Thanks, J. Mom's over the moon.

Jenna: She sent me wedding venues in
Crosslake, MN for a late summer wedding.

Jesus. But the woman moves quickly.

Me: Dad's furious with me.

Jenna: More worried, I think.

Jenna: And he's taking it better today. Rhett
is still ready to defend your honor.

I giggle at that. What honor? All my family members know the truth about Levi and after everything that happened, I don't have much to feel proud about.

Me: We're going out to dinner.

Jenna: So, this is for real? You're going to
stay married to this...hockey player?

Jenna: I think it's hilarious you didn't know who he was. Rhett almost freaked out for a second before he realized y'all got married in Vegas without you knowing what Leif does for a living.

Me: We'll see what happens.

Jenna: What kind of answer is that?

Me: An honest one.

Jenna: You might be able to smooth things over with Rhett too if you give him tickets to a Bolts game.

My doorbell rings and I swear. Exhale. Check my reflection in the mirror hanging over the console in the hallway.

You got this. Everything is fine.

Me: I gotta go. He's here!

Another message comes through from Jenna.

Jenna: Text me later.

Jenna: I want all the deets!

Jenna: Every last one.

Jenna: Have fun!

Jenna: Be safe!

Jenna: Do you have pepper spray?

Jenna: Or a whistle on your keychain?

Considering she bought me both, I text back quickly.

Me: You know I do! Love you, J.

I slide my phone into my purse and pull open the front door.

Leif grins and my heart stutters.

He's wearing relaxed jeans with rips at the knees and a casual, fitted black Henley with the top button undone. His hair is styled. His sneakers are clean. He's casual and...sexier than he should be.

"Hey, Knox," he greets me.

"Leif," I manage.

He dips down and brushes a kiss over my cheek. "You hungry?"

My stomach twists into nervous knots. "Sure."

"I thought we could hit up a taco place I think you'll like. Alberto's."

"Sounds good."

"It's not fancy. They don't even take reservations."

Some of my nerves ease. "Sounds perfect."

He chuckles. I settle my purse over my shoulder, lock the front door, and follow him to his waiting truck. A black Ford F-150.

For some reason, his truck, a reliable, practical, not flashy brand, relaxes me further. I step up and slide onto the passenger seat.

Leif eases himself behind the steering wheel and turns to look at me. He reaches over the center console and takes my hand, flipping my palm up to run his finger over my inner wrist. Over my tattoo. "Not hiding it anymore."

I sigh. "I'm sorry, okay? I know it was messed up to ignore you. I was just...processing."

"I know," he says easily. "And I wasn't saying that to make you feel guilty. I'm happy you're showing off the ink. That you're not ashamed of it."

"I'm not," I confirm, holding up my left hand with my purple ring. "I'm not ashamed of this either. I'm just out of my element. I came to Knoxville to start my life on my own terms. Not be someone's wife."

Leif nods. "I'm not trying to change you, Cam. In fact, I want to know what your terms are." He slides his thumb over my skin again before backing out of the parking spot and pulling onto a main road.

"Why didn't you tell me you're an NHL player?" I ask, changing the subject to focus on him instead of me. I shift in my seat so I can watch his facial expressions.

He sighs, tilting his head back. "Listen, if this is gonna work, we need to be straight with each other, right?"

"Right."

"Okay. Then, I didn't tell you because I liked that you seemed into me for me and not because of what I do for a living."

"I was into you for you," I toss back.

"Exactly." He gives me a quick smile that doesn't reach his eyes. "But most women aren't. It's because I play hockey or because my family is like some hockey royalty family with all us Bang brothers playing the game. Chances are, if a woman isn't into me, she's into one of my brothers."

"There are six of you?" I ask, remembering Mom mentioning Stella's six kids.

"Five boys and a girl," Leif confirms. "We're all in the NHL except Annie but she was a competitive figure skater for years."

"Oh," I breathe out, my memory wandering.

"Dad coaches the juniors now. King's in Oakland with his girl Rory, Jakob's in Portland and now shacked up with his former nanny, Gardenia." I snort. "That woman is a saint for the way she manages and truly loves my twin nephews, Ryder and Rowan. Jensen's settled down in LA with Bailey Walker—"

"The actress?" I interrupt.

"Yep!" Leif nods.

"She won an Oscar."

"I know. None of us could believe Jensen convinced Bailey to give him a shot." He chuckles in a way that lets me know he's kidding. He must be really close with Jensen, kind of like Jenna and me. "Annie lives in New York City and Tanner's in Boston, playing for the Bucks."

"Right," I mutter. "Now that you're painting a picture, I remember little things about your family. Mom would chat with Stella every Christmas break, right after receiving a Christmas card that would highlight what you all were up to."

Leif groans. "Those Christmas cards were always so embarrassing. What were we really up to—besides hockey?"

I chuckle. "My brother played too."

Leif gives me a questioning look.

"Rhett—"

"Coleman," he supplies, nodding slowly. "Had a knee injury his sophomore year of college."

"How do you know that?" I ask.

"Remember Mom and Dad talking about it. He never played again."

"Nope," I confirm. "To be honest, I don't think his heart was in it anymore and the injury was the out he needed." I'd never admitted that to anyone before. And here I am, spilling details of my brother's life with Leif, a professional NHL player. "We all kind of lost interest in the sport after that."

Leif chuckles. "Is that why you didn't recognize me?"

"Hey! To be fair, no one in Vegas did."

"Ouch." He slaps a hand over his heart, and I laugh.

"It's a tough lifestyle. Not for everyone," Leif says. He pulls into a parking lot and cuts the engine. "You like margaritas?"

"You know I do."

"Then you'll like Alberto's," he promises.

I slide from his truck and follow him into the Tex Mex restaurant. The moment the door closes and the vibrant colors, warm atmosphere, and delicious scent of food welcomes us, I know Leif is right. I already like Alberto's.

And I already trust Leif's judgment. I guess my *husband* is a better fit than I originally thought.

———

THE MARGARITAS ARE A GOOD CALL. They relax me, allowing me to speak my mind freely.

"You think it's a red flag that we always need alcohol when we're together?" I ask, holding up my empty margarita glass.

"Probably," Leif agrees. At least he's honest.

"Maybe our next date, we'll stay sober," I suggest.

"Done." His smile widens.

"But tonight..." I trail off, taking a sip of my margarita. "I'll keep the drinks coming."

Leif snickers.

I don't add that tonight, a part of me is hoping I end up in his bed again.

But wait, his mom is in town. Does that mean he should stay at my place?

Argh! What is wrong with me? I told Leif I'm not in love with him and don't want to be a wife, yet...I desperately want to sleep with him again.

This is a confusing disaster in the making.

I suck on the straw to my empty margarita glass and wince when I inhale air.

Leif flags down our server for another round and pops a tortilla chip into his mouth. "You ready to start work on Monday?" He changes the subject.

"Yeah," I say slowly. "I mean, it's not my dream job or anything but it feels good to have a job that will pay the bills."

He leans closer and I wince at how he could interpret that.

"Not that I need money or anything," I continue. "I just want to be independent, you know? And I used most of my savings to pay for my move and the new car. Not that it's new. It's used. But—"

"Cami." Leif places a hand over mine. "You don't have to be nervous. I'm not thinking anything good or bad or judging anything you say. I just want to spend time with you. Get to know you."

"I'm not good at dating," I admit.

"I'm not good at relationships," he shares. "But I want this one with you."

How the hell does he always know what to say?

Our server appears with our food and fresh margaritas. I relax slightly. We dig into our entrees.

"Do you like living in Tennessee?" I ask.

He nods thoughtfully. "It wasn't my first choice, but I like the Thunderbolts. My teammates are solid guys, and the management is one of the best I've ever experienced. Jeremiah Merrick—"

"Isn't he in the Hall of Fame?"

"See! You do know your hockey," Leif beams.

I snort. "Hardly. It's something Rhett mentioned once."

"Yes, he's in the Hall of Fame. He and another former player, Noah Scotch, are the coaches. They're actually family too. Merrick is Scotch's father-in-law. They're tough but fair."

"That's good. What was your first choice?"

"Probably California."

"Because of the surfing?" I guess.

Leif grins. "There's definitely that. And my brother Jensen plays for the Phantoms in LA."

"Right. That's wild that you all play hockey."

"Yeah, but we're all scattered. The good thing is we play each other during the season so it's a built-in time to catch up and grab dinner."

"That's cool."

Leif nods before wrinkling his nose. "Yeah, but I wish I got to see my sister more often."

"Annie? In...New York City," I recall.

"Yep. I see her when we play the Bears though."

"I like that you come from a big family," I admit.

"I love it, too. The only downside is there's very little privacy. We're all up in each other's business and my mother is the worst repeat offender of all."

I shrug. "Trust me, I can relate. No one is more meddlesome, or weighs in with more judgments, than my mom."

"Cheryl does seem intense," Leif replies, searching my eyes. He places down his burrito and cleans his fingers with a napkin. "I thought she'd push back on our marriage, not embrace it."

"She worries about me and thinks if I settle down, I won't be such a wild child."

"You hardly seem wild. Spontaneous and carefree, sure. But not reckless," he surmises.

I sigh. Wrinkle my nose. Admit a version of the truth. "I had a relationship, well, a situationship, that turned sour."

Leif takes a swig of his drink. Clears his throat. His jawline tightens. "Recently?"

"About three years ago."

"Were you together long?"

I snort. "A handful of weeks."

Leif rears back in surprise. He clears his throat. "Something must have happened to leave such a big impression. Especially on your mom." His tone is light. Testing. But his expression is carefully blank. Like he doesn't want me to know what he's really thinking.

I stall, taking another pull from my margarita. "It ended badly." I clear my throat. "My mom doesn't want me to repeat the same mistakes."

Leif nods, but continues to watch me. "Were the mistakes life-altering?"

I bite my bottom lip, half wishing he would come right out and ask me what he wants to know and half wishing he would change the subject completely. "They could have been. And the fact that my reputation was salvaged hangs over my head like a massive warning sign, reminding me that sometimes spontaneity is impulsive. And sometimes carefree *is* reckless."

Leif taps his fingertips against the ledge of the table. "Is that why you don't want to be married to me? Do you think we're more reckless than carefree?"

Shit. I freeze and stare at him. My insides twist and my heart hammers in my temples. I swore to myself that I'd be honest and direct in new relationships. That I would embrace adulting. "I don't know yet."

Leif nods. "That's honest, Cam."

"That's all I can give you," I breathe out.

His arm reaches over the table and his hand settles on mine. My shoulders drop as the warmth of his fingers seeps into my skin. "That's all I need. If we're honest, we can make this work."

I nod and take another sip of my margarita.

But are we supposed to try to make this marriage work? Shouldn't it be intuitive? Shouldn't I feel it and know—deep down—that it's the right call?

As much as I'm enjoying hanging out with Leif, I still can't imagine an entire lifetime with him. Right now, I'm still trying to process my move to Tennessee, my new job starting on Monday, and the fact that I have a husband.

I'm way out of my wheelhouse and I don't possess the calm confidence Leif exudes. I like split decisions and the feeling of euphoria.

Right now, this is starting to feel real.

Genuine and serious and stable.

But not baffling and convoluted and claustrophobic like I imagined.

At least I know, deep down, in my heart, that Leif Bang is a good man. He's a good man who's trying to be an even better husband.

TWELVE

Leif

"I heard Mama Bang is in town!" my teammate River Patton —a guy I've known for years since we played in a handful of tournaments together—announces as I enter the gym.

"She's driving me crazy," I admit as I smack hands with him in greeting.

Last night, she texted me three times while I was on my date with Cami. This morning, she woke me up an hour before my alarm to remind me to start a load of wash. I'm not used to having my mom in my space and I'm giving my brothers a lot of credit for the shenanigans they put up with during her visits.

River chuckles. "I've got nothing. My mom Gayle is a saint and my mothers-in-law..." He whistles low. "Maisy is a dream and Anna gives solid advice."

I shake my head, loving the dynamics of River's family. Between him and his wife Lola, they've done a lot of blending and yet, it works. It's more functional and loving than a lot of other families I know. "Yeah," I agree. "But you've got Axel Daire to watch out for." River's father-in-law, a longtime player with the Thunderbolts, retired at the end of last season. I had the opportunity to play with him for a few months and even though he's not playing the game anymore, his nickname is still Brawler.

At that, River straightens. "Yeah. Axel's fair but you're right, intimidating as hell."

I smirk, although I shouldn't. I don't know anything about Cami's dad. Other than that, he's not a fan of our marriage and wanted to jump on a plane and haul his daughter back to Minnesota.

"That's what I like to hear," Brawler announces, stepping into the gym.

River swears good-naturedly.

Brawler chuckles. "Can't get rid of me, kid. You, Lola, and Mia are coming for dinner tonight, too. So are Jasmine and Johnny."

River shakes hands with him and I watch through narrowed, assessing eyes. I remember the shitstorm that kicked up when Patton knocked up Lola, Brawler's daughter. I think everyone in the League heard about it but given my history with Patton, I got more details than most. Since then, Lola and River had a baby girl, Mia, and tied the knot. Now, everyone is in a good place.

Can't Cami and I achieve that too? I mean, our moms are already friends. We should be able to figure this out. To make it work. And last night, we had a good dinner together. We talked and shared stories. I kissed her good night in front of her apartment door and wished her luck at her new job today. As far as first dates go, it was the realest one I've ever been on and I relished it. Loved spending time with her.

Then, I went home to drink tea with Mom and get an earful on the proper way to fold a fitted sheet.

We can have the happily-ever-after. Hell, if River Patton managed to figure it out, I can too.

"So, your mom's in town?" Brawler asks.

"Mama Bang is no joke," Barnes supplies, picking up heavier weights.

Brawler chuckles. "With five boys in the NHL? I doubt you can pull the wool over her eyes. Heard your brother King is serious with his new girlfriend?"

"She's on a mission for us all to settle down. Now that Mom's retired and...well, she recently lost a close friend...she seems worried that she's not going to be around to see us find our happily-ever-afters," I explain.

River grimaces. Axel quirks an eyebrow.

"Does she have a woman in mind for you?" Axel asks.

Damien drops his weights and sits up on the bench. He eyes me for a moment, silently asking if I'm sure I want to drop the news.

"I got married in Vegas a couple weeks ago," I admit, gripping the back of my neck.

Shock registers on River's and Axel's faces. They both sputter.

Damien laughs. "You have more in common than you give yourselves credit for," he says, gesturing between River and his father-in-law.

"Does your mom know?" River asks.

"Turns out, she was going to set me up with...my wife," I admit.

"No fucking way! You didn't tell me that." Barnes stands and moves closer to our huddle.

"We went on our first date this weekend," I continue.

"Your first date? You're way past that, my man," River points out.

"How'd it go?" Axel presses.

"It went great but...Cami's new in town. She starts a new job today. We're figuring things out," I admit.

Axel crosses his arms over his burly chest. "And this is what you want? Marriage?"

"Is she open to a divorce?" River questions.

"She is. It's me who really wants to give this a shot. She's...different. Lively and smart and funny. I like being with her. I want to make it work." I hate that I sound defensive but why can't anyone just be happy for me that I'm happy? Isn't that enough?

My teammates are quiet for a moment.

And then, Brawler says, "Come for dinner next weekend."

"What?" I sputter, shaking my head.

"All of you." Brawler gestures around the group.

"She's going to need friends in town," River adds.

"Harper's back from Aspen; I'll tell her to reach out," Damien agrees.

I look around the group. "You guys are serious?"

Patton guffaws and hits the back of my head. "You're a Thunderbolt now, Leif. I know we don't have a flashy record but we're a solid group of guys."

"We're a family," Damien states. And then, "We had a good season."

Axel snorts. "We did. I went out on a high." Then he looks at me. "I'll talk to Maisy and we'll organize something for next weekend. Get her to meet the women, to be a part of your life here. Bring your mother too."

I nod, staring at him. "Thank you, Brawler. That means a lot."

"All good, kid," he replies.

"Now let's work out." Damien claps his hands together. "We can't keep skipping the gym to discuss Leif's personal life."

I chuckle and move toward the weight rack. As I move through the exercises, it's with an agility I haven't felt since the end of the season. Everything feels lighter and easier. Smoother.

My team has my back, and I didn't realize how much I needed that. How great it would feel to lean on them.

I hope Cami feels the same way in the future.

"YOU'RE FUCKING MARRIED?" Jake asks. He looks even more serious than usual as he glares at me through the screen.

"Take it easy," my youngest brother, Tanner, tosses out. "Mom says Cami is great."

"Mom would," Jensen mutters, glancing over his shoulder at his girlfriend, Bailey, who is holding back her laughter.

"A Vegas wedding, huh?" my eldest brother Kingston asks.

"I'd never get away with that," Annie laments.

"That's true," I toss out. "Listen, it was obviously not planned but...we're giving it a shot. I can't wait for you all to meet her."

"I hope that happens before your actual wedding," Tanner says.

King chuckles. "With the way Mom's telling it? Y'all will be married—again—by the end of summer."

"The twins are excited," Jake mutters, looking exhausted.

But happy. Since he's settled down with Gardenia, he looks a lot less stressed, which is a good thing.

"I am too," I admit. "And it will be a great opportunity to spend time with Rory, Gardenia, and Bailey," I point out, sticking to the positives.

Annie chuckles. "You're reaching, Leif."

"Hell, I know," I admit.

My siblings laugh.

"You look good, though," Annie adds. "You look happy."

"I am," I say honestly. "I really am. And I truly want to make my marriage work."

"Good for you, man," King tosses out.

Jake and Tanner nod in agreement.

"I'll keep you posted on the wedding details," I say as Mom enters the kitchen. I see her through the screen door leading to my patio. "Mom is out of the shower."

"Oh! I gotta go before she reads me the riot act," Annie says.

"I need to go, too," Jensen says, exchanging another not-so-secret look with Bailey.

Kingston snorts. "How's your visit with Mom going?"

Annie and Jensen sign off.

I sigh. "Honestly, not too bad. I mean, she's driving me nuts with the questions, but all things considered, I think I'm getting off easier than you guys did."

"That's what happens when you marry a stranger," Tanner sounds thoughtful.

"Don't get any ideas," Jake shuts him down.

"But be prepared for Mom," King warns. "While she's happy to visit with Leif, him one-upping her has not taken the wind out of her sails. You and Annie are gonna be next."

King, Jake, and I laugh at Tanner's fearful expression.

"Mom's got the kettle on," I tell them.

My brothers all groan, knowing that means Mom wants to sit down and talk.

"We'll let you go," King says.

I chuckle. "Talk to you guys later." I end the video call.

A few minutes later, Mom steps onto the back porch.

"How was Cami's first day?" Mom takes a seat in the Adirondack chair next to mine and blows on her tea.

"Thanks," I say as she passes me a mug. I love sitting on my back porch, watching dusk fall. It's where I come to relax after a long day. It's also where I take most of my calls, checking in with my family.

Mom's question redirects my thoughts. Cami should have been home from work by now but she still hasn't replied to my text asking her about her first day.

"I don't know. I haven't talked to her yet." I toss a piece of popcorn in the air and catch it in my mouth.

Mom reaches over and grabs a handful from the bowl resting in my lap. "Did you call her?"

"Texted." I sip the tea.

"Hm." She munches on her popcorn.

I look at her. "What does that mean?"

"I didn't say anything."

"You harrumphed."

Mom snorts. "Harrumphed? Not a word I thought you'd use."

I shake my head and take a sip of my water. "You think it's weird she hasn't answered yet?"

Mom shrugs. "Maybe her coworkers took her out for welcome drinks."

I sit up straighter in my chair. I hadn't thought about that. "Do you think they got her drunk?"

"Oh brother," Mom scoffs, taking a drink of her tea. "Leif, she had a whole life before she met you a couple weeks ago."

"I know that."

Mom lifts her eyebrows, calling me out. "You're awfully protective of her."

"So?"

"So, don't scare her off. If you want this to work, you can't smother her."

"I'd hardly call one text smothering."

Mom points at me. "Yet here you sit, emotionally eating."

Now I harrumph and drop back in my seat. "It's Skinny Pop."

Mom laughs. "I made the banana loaf you like."

"With the walnuts?"

Mom nods and grins. "Maybe you can bring some over to Cami. Later. After she's home and has had some time to process her day."

"And you don't think that's smothering?"

"Nope. Food is always seen as a gesture of goodwill."

I consider that and have to agree. I narrow my eyes at Mom. "You're secretly an evil genius, aren't you?"

"No secret part about it," she agrees, tipping her head back as she drops a handful of popcorn into her mouth. "My success ratings can't be beat. I'm three for three."

I laugh at her reference to King, Jake, and Jensen's flourishing romances. "I'm already married."

"And you want to stay that way," she reminds me.

"You'll have a harder time with Annie," I warn her.

"I have different methods for each of my children," she scolds me.

I sigh. "We were invited to dinner next weekend."

"We?"

"Me and Cami and you. One of my teammates who recently retired—"

"Axel Daire," Mom supplies, proving she follows all of

her kids' hockey careers the same way she follows Dad's junior team.

"Correct. He and his wife invited us and a few other of my teammates for dinner."

"They know about Cami?"

I nod.

Mom smiles. "They're trying to welcome her."

"They're good guys."

"You're lucky," she says, relaxing in her chair. "If Cami finds her social circle here, she'll feel more comfortable in Knoxville. She'll feel more confident in her relationship with you. But Leif, this is a big change for her."

"Mom, I got married," I remind her.

She flicks her wrist at me. "Yeah, but nothing phases you the way it does most people. And Cami..." She shakes her head.

"What?"

"Something happened. I don't know what, but Cheryl's hinted at enough to have my Mom sense kicking in."

I frown, thinking about Cami mentioning her bad breakup from three years ago. It's strange she wouldn't have had any serious relationships since, isn't it?

"Something banana bread can't fix?" I aim to keep the conversation light because I don't want to mentally spiral when I don't have facts. When I'm not learning things about Cami from Cami.

Mom smiles gently. "Be patient with her, Leif. There's an extra loaf on the countertop for you to bring her."

"Thanks, Mom." I roll my neck and stare out over the expanse of lawn. It's nearly dusk and the sky is a brilliant mix of pinks and purples. A cotton-candy sky, my brother Tanner used to call it when he was a kid.

"I'm going to call your father," Mom says, standing from her chair.

"He's at camp this week, isn't he?"

"Yes," Mom says, patting the top of my head. "In Michigan."

"Tell him hello for me. And that I've got some good memes I'll be sending his way."

Mom chuckles. "I will."

While Dad is more of the strong and silent type, I like to send him funny memes and reels just for shits and giggles. Every now and then, he'll send one my way too.

The screen door closes and a few minutes later, Mom's voice floats outside as she chats with my dad. They'll be on the phone for a bit, catching up on their days.

I sigh and pull my phone out of my pocket. It's nearly seven PM and still, no word from Cami.

If I don't hear from her in an hour, I'll pass by with Mom's banana bread. It's a good excuse, a thoughtful gesture, and hopefully, another step forward in getting my wife to trust me.

THIRTEEN

Cami

"You never texted after your date," Jenna accuses as I unlock the door to my apartment.

"I was exhausted," I say by way of apology. "Yesterday was busy getting ready for today. Don't you want to hear about my first day of work?"

The door closes behind me and I lock it before toeing off my heels. Ah, that feels better. As my toes sink into the runner that leads from the foyer to the kitchen, I shrug out of the blazer I wore for my first day of work.

My look was professional and polished. A navy skirt suit with a white button-down shirt and nude heels.

You only have one chance to make a favorable first impression. Mom's voice rings in my ears.

"Not as much as I want to hear about Leif. Were you exhausted because your *husband* kept you up late?" Jenna asks and I don't miss the thread of hope in her tone.

I snort. "No. He dropped me at my doorstep and kissed me good night like a gentleman at a very respectable hour."

I move to the fridge and pull out an apple.

"Ugh, boring. Then, why are you so tired?"

"I can't sleep," I admit. I wrinkle my nose as I tell her the truth. "I was nervous about today."

"How'd it go?" Jenna gentles her tone.

"Good. I mean, the job is going to be a snooze fest but also, not too difficult. The coworkers I met are nice. Friendly. A few of them—two guys and a woman—took me out for drinks afterwards."

"That's nice! Cam, at my first day of work, I took coffee orders and spent an absurd number of hours reading through the HR manual."

I chuckle. "This was way better than that."

"So, you feel better about it?"

I nod, glancing at the stack of sketchbooks I pulled out last night after my date with Leif. Rattled, nervous, and confused, I was up late sketching. Drawing all the things I can't put into words. But drawing has always been thera-peutic for me. Give me a pencil and a blank piece of paper and I can create something with all the feelings that bottle up inside. From all the thoughts I'm not sure how to express or share. "Yeah," I tell Jenna.

"Good! I'm glad you met some new people today."

"Me too. The woman, Maria, is really nice. She's older and has a two-year-old daughter. Her husband is in the National Guard and is deployed for the next six months."

"Wow. That must be tough."

"Right? But her mom is staying with her, so she has the extra support to focus on her career. She became a certified CPA a few months ago."

"What about the guys?" Jenna asks.

"Tarek and Sam," I mention my male coworkers. "Seem like good guys. No red flags."

Jenna snorts. "Glad you got all of that from a few drinks."

I shrug. "It felt good. Normal. Like a regular thing to do."

"It is good. And normal," my sister stresses. "You missed out on too many opportunities to mingle and meet people after things went sideways with Levi. You cut yourself short."

"Yeah," I whisper, sitting down at the kitchen island. It's a small island with two barstools but perfect for me. I take a bite of my apple. "Do you think I'm doing that again?"

"Cutting yourself short?"

"I married a stranger," I remind her.

"I don't think Leif is anything like Levi. I don't think most men are."

I roll my eyes. "No, most men aren't infamous rockstars."

Jenna giggles. "Leif is a professional hockey player though. Can't you just date a normal guy—like a teacher or a dentist?"

I sigh. "I clearly have a type."

Jenna chuckles.

"But I don't want to miss out on opportunities, on social experiences, because I'm a *wife*."

"Then, don't," Jenna says, as if it's that easy.

I roll my eyes. "Right. Because Mom continued to explore her career options when she married Dad."

"Mom also had three kids back-to-back. You're not even living with your husband, Cam. You're not obligated to go to all his hockey games and become a WAG. You're figuring things out, one day at a time. Just, give him, give this a chance. If that's what you want to do. You said you do. Is it because of Mom? And the way she jumped on the Leif Bang wagon?"

"Partly," I admit. "You should have seen her face, Jenna.

She was so relieved, and I didn't want to disappoint her again."

Jenna sighs. "That's not a good enough reason to stay in a marriage."

"It's convenient," I point out.

Jenna scoffs. "That's even worse."

"I know. But partly, there is something between Leif and me. I had fun on our date. He is a good guy. If I wasn't married to him, I'd date him in a heartbeat."

Jenna snorts.

"It's bananas," I mutter.

"Cam, you can define what it means to be a wife, what it means to be married, for you and Leif. You don't have to follow the example set by Mom and Dad or anyone else. You set the terms. You and Leif make the rules."

"You have a point," I concede.

"I always do. Anyway, I'm meeting my book club tonight."

I grin, loving that Jenna has maintained a book club with the same girls from college for over four years. "Have fun."

"Thanks! We read a paranormal romance—*The Hunted* with vampire Navy SEALS—by S.B. Alexander this month. I'm glad you had a great first day, Cam."

"Me too. Talk to you later."

"'Bye." Jenna ends the call.

I toss down my phone and bite into my apple. Then, I pull the refrigerator door open again, wondering what I should eat for dinner. I'm not much of a cook and I'm debating between cereal and an omelette when the doorbell rings.

Who would be here at this time of night? Hell, I barely know anyone in this city.

A knock sounds. "Knox? You home?"

Leif. I can't stop the smile that curls my lips. Is he checking in on me? I like that he stopped by. I stride toward the front door and pull it open.

Leif shuffles back half a step, his eyes dropping down my frame and back to my eyes. "You look...very professional."

I grin. "You wanted to say librarian, didn't you?"

"More powerhouse CEO."

I shake my head and step to the side. "Come on in. What are you doing here?"

He holds up a Tupperware. "Bringing baked goods. For your first day."

"Oh! That was...thoughtful."

He smiles. "Homemade too. Mom made it."

"Please thank Stella for me." I close the door and take the Tupperware from his hands. "Perfect timing too. I was just wondering what I should eat for dinner."

Leif frowns. "It's banana bread."

"Mm. Excellent!" I hope it has walnuts. It will pair nicely with tea. Dinner problem solved! "Want some? I'm thinking banana bread and tea."

Leif looks amused. "Sure." He follows me into the kitchen and slides onto a barstool while I turn on the kettle. "How was your first day?"

"Surprisingly good," I admit, turning to face him. I drop my elbows to the island and lean forward. Note that his eyes flicker to the buttons on my blouse before flying back to my face.

I bite my bottom lip to keep from smiling. I like that Leif checks me out. I want him to be attracted to me.

His presence—normal and thoughtful and relaxed— puts me at ease. Jenna was right; Leif and I will make the terms of our marriage. Right now, I really am happy to see him.

"Good." He nods. "I got worried when you didn't reply to my text."

I squint, recalling his message just as we ordered drinks at the bar. "Oh, sorry. Some colleagues took me out for celebratory drinks and then my sister Jenna called."

Leif nods, tapping his fingertips against the ledge of the island. "Where'd you go for drinks?"

I frown. Is he giving me the third degree? "McCullen's Pub."

Leif tilts his head. "Ah, I know where that is. Well, there's a sports pub, called Corks, that's really good and also walking distance to your office. Just, in the opposite direction."

I relax as he tosses out the suggestion. Nope, he's just being considerate and making conversation. "Good to know. Thanks."

"No problem."

The kettle whistles and I fix our tea as Leif moves around my kitchen to find a knife and cutting board. He cuts thick slices of banana bread before pulling open the refrigerator door and rummaging around.

"You need more food," he tells me.

I wrinkle my nose. "I'm not much of a cook."

"I can see that by the overwhelming number of condiments and nothing else," he mutters, grabbing the cream cheese.

I stick my tongue out at him, and he smirks.

"I'm an okay cook," he continues, "so I can do that when we move in together."

I arch an eyebrow. "That seems rushed, don't you think?"

Leif shrugs. "We're married, Cam. And I want us to do this for real."

I bite the corner of my lip.

I like that he's here. It's comfortable, the two of us moving around my kitchen with ease. It feels like we've done this before even though it's the first time. But I just moved into my new place—my first grown-up apartment—and I'm not ready to give that up yet.

I clear my throat and change the subject instead. "How was your day?"

He grins, silently calling me out on my not-so-subtle tactic. "Not bad. I got a workout in. Some of the team was around too. Hey, if you're not busy next weekend, one of my former teammate's Axel invited us to dinner at his place."

"Us?" I pull up short. "Do they know about us?"

"Being married?"

I nod.

"Yeah." His eyebrows tug together. "That's okay, right? I mean—"

"Yes, of course," I rush to reassure him. To gain some footing in this conversation. "I just don't know how to navigate this with you."

"I know." He turns so he's facing me. He places a strong, steady hand on my hip. "We'll figure this out together, okay? I told Axel I'd check with you, but I'd like to have dinner with some of the team next weekend. It will give you a chance to meet them, get to know their wives and families."

I smile at the idea of meeting more people in Knoxville. "Okay."

"My mom is going to tag along too," Leif adds.

I grin. "It will be nice to get to know Stella better."

Leif snorts. "You say that now."

"She can't be worse than Cheryl. I have to show you the venues she's sending me from Crosslake."

Leif flexes his fingers on my hip, and I fight the urge to lean into him. Just because my body is insanely attracted to his doesn't mean I can turn off my brain when he's around. We need to explore this carefully. Like adults.

"We can have whatever kind of wedding you want. And if you don't want one, that's okay too." Leif leans forward to press a kiss to my cheek before resuming his job of spreading cream cheese on the banana bread. "Also, this weekend, we can go out for dinner. I can show you around the city."

"I'd like that," I say, meaning it. I do want to learn more about the city I now call home. And, if I'm being honest, it will be a lot more enjoyable to explore with Leif by my side. I know I'll have fun with him.

I focus on making our tea, on enjoying this moment with him, on completing my first day of work. Little by little, I relax and begin to consider my future with Leif.

I certainly like spending time with him. I'm one-hundred percent attracted to him. I even want to spend time with his mom and meet his teammates next weekend.

Just because our start wasn't typical doesn't mean we don't stand a chance. We can make our own rules. We can do this on our own terms.

Leif stays for a few hours, and we hang out like a normal couple. We sip our tea, talk about our college years, and sit too close to each other on the couch watching a rerun of *How I Met Your Mother*.

When it nears eleven PM, Leif kisses me good night. His lips are soft on mine. My hands find his hips and hold. Our connection is intense and leaves me dizzy. Breathless.

After Leif leaves, I make a fresh cup of tea. Then, I sit at the kitchen island and open my sketchbook. I flip through the pages of gowns I've created over the past six months. They're all fashionable designs, with delicate details, for formal events.

My fingers itch, wanting to create, as I pick up the pencil.

As I press the point into the paper, my mind clears, my worries ease, and my hands know what to do. I stay up too late, until the side of my hand is smudged with shades of gray. But the wedding dress I draw is the dress of my heart.

It's unlike any design I've ever created and it's exactly the type of gown I'd wear.

It's strapless with a full skirt and a simple veil.

It's lacy, elegant, yet understated. It's beautiful.

And for the first time, I can envision myself wearing it, walking down the aisle, and exchanging vows with Leif Bang.

FOURTEEN

Leif

"Hi, Cami!" Mom pulls open the front door to my home.

"Hi, Stella." Cami hugs Mom hello.

"How was your second week of work?" Mom asks, leading Cami into the kitchen where I'm concocting drinks before we head to Brawler's house for dinner.

"Busy," Cami says, sliding onto a barstool at my kitchen island. She glances around the space, and I realize it's the first time she's been here. Over the past week, I dropped by her apartment, or we met out, in the city. "I like your place."

"He did an okay job, but I really elevated it since I've been in town," Mom chimes in.

Cami grins as I roll my eyes. "Thanks, Cami." I place a mojito in front of her before adding a fresh mint sprig.

She picks up the glass and bites the corner of her mouth. "I didn't realize I married a mixologist."

Mom straight up cackles before sliding onto the barstool

next to Cami's. She picks up her drink. "Cheers, Cami. I want to hear all about work."

"Thanks, Stella. And thank you for the banana bread. It was delicious and I really appreciated the walnuts," Cami replies, clinking her glass against Mom's before taking a sip. "Mm, this is good, Leif."

"Thanks. I hope you ate something other than banana bread for dinner this week." I lean against the countertop across from Mom and Cami and cross my ankles at my feet.

Cami grins. "I only had it for dinner twice."

"Leif! Cook for your wife." Mom scowls at me.

"This week flew by, Stella. Between work, which is boring but bearable, and getting to know my new coworkers, who are so much more fun than I thought accountants would be, the days have been hectic."

"I'm glad you have good colleagues," Mom replies thoughtfully.

"I really like this one woman, Maria. And two of the men on my team, Sam and Tarek. Tarek's become my de facto mentor. We made plans to go to happy hour next Friday." Cami looks at me. I really hope this isn't her asking my permission or something equally as weird. "Do you want to come?"

Oh. I grin. She's inviting me. To meet her friends— colleagues, whatever. "Yeah, I'd love to." I want to learn all the pieces of her life. While we've certainly started to find our footing over the past week and spent most of the weekend exploring Knoxville together—our conversations during the workweek have consisted of hanging out and watching television, or texts and nightly phone calls.

The more I learn about my wife, the more I can't believe we ended up together. She truly is perfect for me. I'll have to ask Jensen what the odds are of ending up with your soul mate. And then, to refine the odds when the woman is plucked out from a random night in Vegas.

Mom's eyes dart between us and she smiles.

"Cool," Cami says, taking another sip of her drink. "How was your week?" she asks Mom.

"Oh, it was wonderful. As you can see, I got Leif's house in order." Mom gestures around the space, which looks exactly like it did when she arrived.

Cami catches my sigh and fights a giggle.

"I've cooked a bunch. There are meals in the freezer." She looks pointedly at me. "Maybe invite your wife over for dinner."

"For sure," I mutter. "It will be real romantic with you sitting in between us."

Mom laughs, hardly deterred. "And I got to meet some of Leif's teammates, which is always nice. A few of them—like River Patton and his Coach, Jeremiah Merrick—I've known for years. River played in the same circuits as Leif and my other son, Jensen. And Jeremiah and my husband, Lars, go way back, so it was nice to see him again and catch up with his wife, Leanne. We had lunch yesterday. She has the two most adorable grandchildren, Emmaline and Fox."

"You do too. Ryder and Rowan," I remind Mom before she gets any ideas and tries to suggest children since Cami and I are technically married.

Mom flicks her wrist at me dismissively. "A little girl would be nice."

Cami chokes on her mojito. Naturally, Mom slaps her on the back.

"Mom," I mutter, passing Cami a napkin.

"Thanks," Cami says, dabbing at the tears under her eyes.

"Sorry, Camille. I wasn't insinuating anything." My mother is a terrible liar.

"Really?" I give her a look.

She shrugs and gives me a sheepish look back. "Are you okay, love?"

"I'm fine, Stella." Cami manages a chuckle.

"All right, I better finish dressing before we leave." Mom slides off her barstool and retreats to my guest room.

"I'm relieved we're already married or I'm sure you'd bolt," I tell Cami.

She grins at me. "I really like your mom. From the mother-in-law horror stories I've heard, I think I hit the lottery with Stella." She wrinkles her nose. "Too bad you can't say the same for Cheryl."

"Ah! You speak too soon." I pull my phone from my back pocket and pull up a text exchange I now have going with my mother-in-law. I slide it across the island so Cami can read it.

"Oh, God," she groans. "She got your number?"

I laugh easily. "It's fine."

"She's messaging you constantly. Are these...cake flavors?"

"She offered to do our cake tasting for us. We're getting married August 21 in Crosslake."

Cami's mouth drops open. "Leif, you have to put a stop to this."

"Me?" I shake my head, grinning. "She's your mom, Cami."

Cami groans again and drops her face into her hand.

I round the island to stand closer to her. Take her hand and hold it against my chest. "Look at me, babe."

She does. Instantly, I'm captured by her big, blue eyes. "I want what you want. Whatever that is, I'm good with it."

She makes a sound in the back of her throat I can't decipher. It's a little laughter, a little frustration, a little confusion. "I do like Crosslake. We used to go there every summer for a

week when I was a kid. Rhett would make bets with Jenna
and me over who would catch the biggest fish."

"Let me guess—you won."

Cami gives me a look. "Obviously. Rhett was too techni-
cal, and Jenna got bored after an hour. But I was committed."
She pauses when she says the word and her eyes scan mine
sharply. She smirks. "I guess sometimes, when I commit, I do
follow through."

I laugh and bend down to press a kiss to her mouth. "I'm
glad to hear that, Knox."

"You should be," she tosses back, lacing my fingers with
hers. "But if Mom becomes too much..."

"She's fine. It's all fine. We'll...figure it out."

"And tonight, I'll meet your teammates."

"And next week, I'll meet your coworkers."

Cami nods. "You know, this is the most functional relationship I've ever been in. Not that I have a lot of experience
to draw from but...we're doing a bang-up job."

"Definitely bang-up," I agree.

She groans. "I'm so not taking your last name when we do
this again." She gestures between us, her purple ring flashing.

I gasp. "No? But think of all the jokes and puns you'll
miss out on hearing."

"I'll hear them by association." She pinches my side.

I laugh. "Fair enough, babe. I like you as Cami Coleman,
anyway."

"Not to change the subject. Or rush things..."

"But?" I frown, wondering where she's going with this.

Cami twirls on her barstool, framing one of my thighs in
between her knees. She lowers her voice. "Any chance I can
convince you to stay at my place tonight?"

I suck in an inhale. Yes, I realize how silly it sounds since,
you know, we're married. But Cami and I haven't had sex

again since that first night and it's been hard as fuck to take things slowly with her. Especially when my blood sings and my body reacts every time she's near.

The scent of her shampoo, the shape of her neck, the sound of her voice—everything about her turns me on.

I bite my bottom lip, trying to hold back my smirk. "Mama Bang will think we're—"

"Don't say it!" She giggles.

I lean down to kiss her again. "I'd love to stay at your place tonight. I'm happy you asked."

"Good." She tilts up her face to kiss me back.

The second her tongue peeks through and drags along the seam of my lips, I part them. Our kiss morphs from PG to PG-13 and I can't help but drop a palm to her ass and push her closer into my frame.

Cami drops my hand to hold my hips and I slant her head, kissing her deeper. Her chest rises, pushing up into mine and I wish we didn't have dinner plans, and my mother wasn't here, so I could lay her out on the kitchen island and do all the things I've been dreaming up since the first time I had her.

I'd take it slow. Then fast. Then all over again until we're both too drained to move.

"Good God, you two! Get a room!" Mom hollers, announcing her arrival back into the communal space.

It's literally the fucking worst when your own mother cockblocks you. I groan and pull away from Cami.

Meanwhile, she drops her face and covers her mouth with her hand, trying to conceal her laughter.

Mom hears the peals of Cami's giggles and joins in.

"You ready to go?" Mom asks.

Cami nods and slips off the barstool. "I'll just use the bathroom first."

"First door on your right." I point down the hallway.

Cami excuses herself and Mom gives me a pointed look.

"What?" I ask, taking a sip of my drink.

"That escalated," Mom comments.

I snort and shake my head. "How long are you staying for?"

Mom laughs at that but doesn't answer. Instead, she relocates to the foyer and slips into her sandals.

Five minutes later, we're on our way to Brawler's house and I can't tamp down the anticipation that fills my limbs about the possibilities of tonight. I'm not nervous; I'm proud. I want my teammates to know my wife. I can't wait to introduce her to Dad and my brothers and sister. I want everyone I care about to know the woman I'm going to spend my life with.

FIFTEEN

Cami

"You must be Cami!" A friendly woman with beach blonde waves and bright blue eyes opens the door. She's smiling warmly and I like her instantly. She kind of reminds me of an older, more mature Jenna.

"I am," I say, hugging her hello.

"I'm Maisy." Maisy hugs me back.

"Thank you so much for having us tonight," I say, stepping aside so Stella and Leif can greet Maisy.

While they say hello, I'm intercepted by a giant of a man with dark eyes and a man-bun. I grin. "You must be Brawler."

He smirks. "I like that my name precedes me." Brawler pulls me into a hug.

"Thanks for inviting me." I hand him the bottle of wine I picked up. Leif also has a few bottles but I wanted to bring something too. I wanted Leif to know that I'm making an effort to connect with his teammates.

"Thanks, Cami. You didn't have to bring anything." Brawler

places the wine bottle on a countertop. "Let me introduce you to everyone." He guides me deeper into his home. It's an open-concept floor plan and I love how the spaces blend together.

When we enter the living room, two hulking men—obviously teammates of Leif's—stand. Two women chatting by the fireplace turn toward us and come closer. "This is Damien—"

"Team Captain," I say.

Damien grins. "You got it. Good to meet you, Cami." He holds out a hand and I shake it. "This is my fiancée, Harper."

"I still love hearing that!" Harper singsongs, pulling me into a hug. "It's so good to meet you. I'm in the midst of wedding planning so we can compare notes."

I smile at her friendliness. "I'd like that."

"This is my daughter, Lola," Brawler continues.

"Hi, Cami!" Lola hugs me hello. Just then, a little cry rings out. "Oops, Mia's awake. Excuse me." She darts down a hallway.

"I'm River." The tough-looking guy with tattoos stretching from his neck to his knuckles says, holding out a hand.

I exchange a handshake. "I've heard of you."

"Uh-oh," Harper teases.

I blush and shake my head. "No, nothing bad. Stella was just saying how nice it was to see you again since you used to play in the same circuit as Leif and Jensen."

River nods. "It's been a long time, but Stella is a trip."

"She definitely is," I agree.

Damien laughs. "What are you drinking?"

"I got it," Brawler says, moving toward the kitchen to get drinks.

"Oh, thanks!" I call after him.

"I know Cole and Beau are going to be disappointed they missed meeting you," Harper says, referencing two more of Leif's teammates. "They're practically brothers-in-law since Beau's little sister Bea is dating Cole."

"And they're in Mexico at the moment for their Gran's birthday." River shakes his head, looking amused. "Gran's turning ninety-three—"

"Or ninety-four?" Damien asks.

River shrugs. "She's in her nineties, man, and the fact that she can still rally and get all her grandkids to take a trip to Mexico is the biggest flex I've ever seen."

We all laugh. "I hope I'm like that in my nineties," I admit.

"You and me both," Stella agrees, coming into our huddle.

Brawler hands me a glass of wine and I relax. Little pockets of conversation break out. When I look over my shoulder, Leif's eyes are on me, watching. I give him a smile and he grins back, his blue eyes dancing.

We're doing it. And it feels good. Right.

"It's crazy to think you two married on a fluke," Harper comments.

I look at her, waiting for an explanation.

She looks between me and Leif and then leans closer, lowering her voice. "He looks at you like you've known each other for years. Like he's smitten."

"You think so?" I ask, wondering if she's being truthful or just trying to make me feel better.

"Yeah, I do." Harper's tone is serious, her expression certain.

"I hope so," I whisper back, grateful to feel a connection to someone here.

"Me too," she agrees, grinning. "And I love your purple ring."

I hold out my hand and we both laugh.

When I look up, Leif is still watching me. And I realize Harper's right, he does look smitten. I wonder if I look at him the same way.

It's only been a handful of weeks but the way I feel for Leif is different. At the end of the day, I look forward to speaking with him. When too many hours pass, I find myself wondering about his day. I get excited when he comes over or we make plans.

Is this what dating is supposed to feel like? Is this the beginning of falling in love?

God, I hope so.

⌐——

I'M TIPSY the moment I pull Leif into my apartment.

Stella, bless her, grabbed a ride home with River, Lola, and Mia since they were going in the same direction as Leif's place. In fact, she seemed giddy at the thought of Leif and me shacking up.

Another nonconventional reaction I'm embracing because for the last third of the evening at the Daires' house, all I could think about was getting my husband naked.

Leif closes the door behind him and locks up. When he turns to face me, I've already whipped off the dainty, floral camisole I wore to dinner, and I'm working on the zipper of my skirt.

Leif freezes, his eyes drinking me in. Then, he's at my side, stilling my hands, touching my waist, and stepping into my frame. "Don't rush tonight, Knox. Tonight, I want to enjoy every inch of you."

I shiver from the promise in his tone, from the gravity shading his eyes. "Leif..." His name is a whisper on my lips.

He sweeps my hair behind my shoulders, gathers it in his large hand, and twists, angling my head as his mouth drops to mine. His kiss lingers and we take our time, our tongues meeting in languid strokes. I tug on the hem of his shirt and manage to roll it up his body until he reaches behind his neck and tugs it off, dropping it on the floor.

Then, my palms are on the smooth skin of his chest, my fingers inching down to trace the ridges of his abs. His arms wrap around me, one hand grabbing my ass as he presses me against him.

He's already hard, already wanting, and the knowledge that I can turn on a man like Leif Bang is an ego boost that hits like a shot of adrenaline. I pop the button on his jeans, he slides down the zipper of my skirt, and within minutes, we're clad in our underwear, our bodies pressed together.

This time, our coming together is different. We're not drunk. We're not even tipsy. We're just us, inhaling each other's exhales and learning the map of each other's bodies.

My hands track over Leif's strong back, my fingertips brushing the colors of the sunset. Leif's mouth trails down the column of my neck, his fingers hooking under the thin straps of my bra. Then, he lifts me. He does so easily, and I wrap my legs around his waist as he walks into my bedroom, one hand gripping my ass, the other splayed wide in the center of my back.

He lays me in the center of my bed. Gently.

He looms over me. A giant, taking up all the space, the air, of the room and commanding my entire focus. I shiver from the pure desire flaring in his eyes.

And I don't compare the man before me to Levi Rousell. I don't even think of Levi. Because there is no comparison.

Leif Bang blots out my past mistakes, my greatest source of shame, my inability to fully trust the man I'm with, and allows me to let go.

To surrender to the moment.

I reach for him, and he comes gladly, settling his strong, ripped, gorgeous body between my thighs. He kisses me deeply. His touch is sure and thorough. The most incredible man I've ever met with the bluest eyes I've ever seen makes love to me like I'm worthy of every single thing he has to offer. Like I'm worthy of him.

He removes my bra slowly, rolls my panties down my legs, and kisses his way down. He takes his time enjoying my breasts, pulling them in between his lips one at a time. He flicks his tongue over my nipples, trails kisses over the soft swells. He licks a path down my abdomen, brushes his fingertips over the ink on my ribs.

I'm so turned on, I can feel the heat gathering between my legs. I arch my back each time his lips make contact with my sensitive skin, wanting his mouth to claim my core with a desperation that borders on needy.

But Leif wasn't kidding. Tonight, he is savoring me, and we share another moment. Another instant when time seems to stop.

My fingers grip the hair on the side of his head. One of my legs is tossed over his shoulder, the other bent at the knee. His large hand grips my inner thigh, the other slips underneath my ass. I look down at him and bite my bottom lip to keep from calling out.

I'm hot and achy. Keyed up and desperate. It feels like I'm about to unravel and I've never wanted it as badly as I do tonight.

Leif's eyes are hooded. Electric blue and an arrow to my

heart. "You're it for me, Knox." His voice is a rasp. A confession. A promise.

And then, his mouth drops to my core, and he licks a path through my slick folds before sucking softly—deliciously—on my clit. And I see stars.

"Leif." His name is a prayer, an exaltation, on my lips.

My hips come off the bed and my eyes squeeze shut.

Leif holds my thighs open as he licks and nibbles and worships the most sensitive part of my body in a way no man has bothered before. It's a matter of mere heartbeats before I'm ready to shatter.

Need coils in my lower abdomen. Pressure builds. My heat rolls and the sound of Leif smacking his lips is a reminder that I'm so damn wet for him. Dripping.

He slides two fingers inside and curls his finger.

"Oh, God," I cry out.

He pumps them slowly.

I grasp at my duvet cover, fisting it in my hand.

His mouth sucks at my clit, his tongue flattening against the little bundle of nerves.

And I shatter.

"Leif..." I reach for him with my free hand. But he continues his ministrations, wringing the orgasm from my body and allowing me the time to crest and coast on the pleasure it provides.

It's intense and wonderful. It's colors and light. It's unlike any moment I've ever shared with a man, and it wraps me in the knowledge I've been seeking.

This is right. Leif is good. We're meant to be.

Fate. Kismet. Destiny.

I believe it. I believe in him. Us.

I arch my back one final time before pressing my body back into the mattress. Leif smirks before kissing his way back up my body. My skin feels hot, feverish. His mouth is cool, a salve. When his lips take mine, I kiss him deeply, passionately, and he enters me easily.

My body is ready for him. Wants him. Hell, needs him.

"Oh, fuck, Cami," he mutters as he bottoms out. His fingers push my hair out of my face and he looks at me, truly sees me, while our bodies our joined. We're connected on every level possible and it's heady, exhilarating, *home.* "You're it for me."

"You're mine," I reply, closing my eyes and pulling him closer for another kiss.

Leif begins to move, pumping in and out, rolling his hips, and setting a pace that is both languid and delicious. He makes love to me like I'm a treasure and I savor him because I know he is.

Wearing only my purple ring, I come together with my husband and know in my heart that I'm starting to fall for him.

I relish knowing this isn't a mistake. No, being with Leif is only the beginning.

We come together, ride out that delicious wave, and collapse beside each other, breathless and giddy.

"Cami, that was..." Leif trails off, his eyes wild.

"Thanks for not giving up on us, Leif."

He shakes his head slightly, his lips pressing together. He grabs my hip and pulls me closer, until my mouth can press a kiss to the hollow of his throat. "I'll never give up on us, Cami."

The reassurance in his voice makes me smile.

Against all odds, Leif gave me something real to trust in. Him. Even though I don't deserve it. Even though I've spent three years faltering and confused about how to move forward with a man. I'm doing it with my

husband, and I'm not scared. I'm emboldened.
Confident.

I'm falling in love.

I bite my bottom lip as Leif hugs me to his chest. We fall
asleep in each other's arms, and I feel safe. Home.

I wake to the sound of dripping water. Slow, steady,
continuous.

At first, I think it's rain but then, I realize that it's coming
from inside my apartment. Shaking myself awake, I sit up in
bed and look around my bedroom.

"Leif." I give him a little nudge.

"Hmm?" He turns, one hand bent behind his head. His
bare chest is on full display and his lips are pursed in sleep.

I take a moment to admire him because I'm human.
Lightly, I trace his mouth. "You're beautiful."

His lips curve into a smile. His eyes blink open. "Love
waking up to your face, Knox."

I smile back. "I'm glad to hear that because I think we
have a situation."

Sleep fades from Leif's eyes at the truth in my tone. He
sits up, his body now alert. "What's that sound?"

"So you hear it, too?" I snort. Then groan. "We must have
a leak somewhere."

"Stay here." He slips from bed, and I get a glorious
second to admire his ass. Then, he pulls on his jeans. Boo.

Leif pads into the hallway and I wrap myself in a robe,
moving to follow him.

When I step beside him by the kitchen, I note he's
looking up. I follow his gaze and snort.

Water is dripping from the ceiling, splattering to the floor
right in front of my kitchen sink.

"The apartment above you must have a busted pipe," Leif
comments.

"I like that you know these things," I muse.

He looks at me. "Are you upset?"

"About what?" I shrug. "It's just a leak. We're not getting carried away in floodwaters."

Leif smirks. Tosses an arm around my shoulders. "Sometimes, I think we're too much alike, Cami Coleman."

"Is that a good or bad thing?" I snuggle closer.

"Still deciding," he admits honestly.

I snort and press a kiss to the side of his chest.

He tightens his hold on me. "You know what this means, right?"

"What?"

"You're moving in with me, my wife."

"I..." I trail off. Because I don't hate the idea. In fact, a tiny thrill shoots down my spine. I bite the corner of my mouth and glance around the space Mom and I decorated. "I only lasted here a month."

Leif snickers. He drops a kiss to the top of my head. "If you're not ready to move in, we'll set you up someplace else," he offers like the gentleman he is.

"No, it's okay. I want to move in with you."

"Yeah?" His eyes dance.

I nod. Smile. Commit. "Yes."

Leif lets out an exhale. "I'm glad to hear it, Cam."

I frown. "Really?" I didn't think us living apart was bothering him.

He nods. "This means my mom will go home and give us a break."

I sputter out a laugh at Leif's reasoning and realize I would feel the exact same way. We stand in my leaky kitchen, half naked, and fold over with laughter.

And I relish that too.

SIXTEEN

Leif

"Cook for her, Leif! She deserves a homemade meal when she comes home from work," Mom reminds me as she rolls her suitcase toward the front door.

Cami tosses me a smirk and I stifle a laugh. Crazy that I get married in Vegas and my mother sides with my new wife on nearly all things.

"I will, Mom," I say, opening my arms.

Mom gives me a big hug. "I had fun visiting you."

"Thanks for coming." I kiss her temple. Even though she's meddlesome and quirky and doesn't understand boundaries, I love my mom with every fiber in my being and I enjoyed having her stay with me more than I'll ever admit. "I can drive you to the airport, you know."

Mom laughs and pulls away to Cami. "I like to keep my independence," she replies, waving to the Uber driver who idles in my driveway.

"We know it." I pick up her suitcase and walk it to the waiting car.

Mom and Cami exchange a few more words before Cami gives her one last hug. It shouldn't affect me the way it does—watching Mom and Cami interact, witnessing them get along—but I like it. I'm grateful that my wife and my mom have hit it off the way they have. That while I've learned to navigate a marriage, my mom welcomed Cami as a daughter-in-law with open arms and thoughtful advice. Even more, Cami was receptive to it.

It almost seems too good to be true. But everything about Cami and me has been unexpected and unconventional. Why should this be any different?

"See you soon, Mom," I say, helping Mom into the car and making sure she's settled up with the Uber driver.

Cami and I stand on the front porch and wave good-bye to Mom until the car's taillights turn the corner.

Then I turn toward my girl and grin. "You ready to unpack?"

She smiles back. It's genuine and lights her face up. "Did you designate half the closet for me?"

I laugh. "Babe, I never even filled half the closet. I've only been here six months and, I'm not that complicated of a guy. I don't have fashion sense like Hudson. You take up all the space you need."

"Wow." Cami's eyes widen and she drops her mouth open in mock surprise. "A husband who cooks and gives me the whole closet?" She tugs on my shirt and pulls me flush against her frame. Grinning up at me, I'm struck by how gorgeous she is. "Seems like I hit the husband lottery with you, Ten."

I snort and palm her ass. I lift her easily and she twines

her legs around my waist. I squeeze the tops of her thighs, relieved my mother is gone. "I'm good at other things too."

Cami smirks. "Like what?"

"I could show you." I carry her into the house and kick the door closed behind me.

"Where?" She glances around our place, her eyes lingering on the kitchen island.

I chuckle. "You're something else, Knox." I stride toward the kitchen island and place her on the edge. Then, I brace my hand behind her, splaying my fingers, as I lean into my beautiful wife and kiss her senseless.

She tightens her legs on my waist, digging the heels of her feet into my ass and dragging my hard cock along her core as she leans back.

It's as if we've finally realized we're alone. That it's just me and her and this house. Our marriage.

Our clothes come off quickly. Our mouths meet in a frenzy. Our hands are desperate, our touches rushed. We clash perfectly, two free spirits colliding on a slab of marble in the middle of the damn day.

My wife makes sounds I get off on. Her body responds to my touch beautifully. I unravel under the watchful gaze of her hooded eyes and wonder how the hell I got so lucky.

How the hell is this my life?

Tugging her off the island, I lay her down in the middle of the damn dining room but she turns the tables, pushing me onto my back so she can climb on top and ride me. Fuck, she does it with abandon.

"That's it, baby," I coax her, my palm gliding up and down the back of her thigh.

My girl finds her rhythm, she chases her pleasure, and I have the immense pleasure of watching her reach the peak and fall over the edge. "You're too fucking much, Cami."

She rolls her hips slowly, grinding her pussy against me until I cry out her name, jack my hips up, and spill inside her. Then, she collapses on top of me and I hold her against my chest. We're sticky and messy and deliriously sated.

"I never knew it could be like this," she murmurs.

"Me neither," I admit, brushing my lips over her silky hair.

"Does this part last?"

"I fucking hope so."

"Me too," she murmurs.

We lay like that for a long stretch of time before we both relocate to the bathroom. Under the hot stream of water in the shower, we come together again. Slowly this time. I press my wife against the cool glass of the shower and shadow her back with my frame. Through the steam, I can make out her outline in the mirror hanging across from the shower. I watch her reflection, the way her lips part, the heaviness of her breasts as they spread along the glass, how her hand clasps me behind the neck and pulls my head down. I pump in and out of her from behind slowly and witnessing it unfold through the mirror is one of the most erotic experiences of my life.

Taking her hand in mind, I move her fingers over her clit in slow, even circles. "Look how perfect you are." My voice is low. A growl. I nip her ear and she turns her head, finding us in the mirror.

Cami whimpers.

I apply more pressure to her fingertips and her breath hitches.

"Leif."

"Come for me, baby." I move her fingers faster. Thrust into her quicker. "I want to feel you come apart on my cock."

"Fuck," she mutters, unable to look away.

I find her gaze in the mirror and hold it. It's hazy now. We're surrounded by steam and the shower takes on an ethereal quality that reminds me of that first night—in the club.

"Oh, God, Leif. I'm coming," Cami cries out, shuddering. I hold her closer, banding an arm around her stomach to keep her upright as her knees give out. When she gets her legs under her, I lace my fingers with hers and place both of our joined hands on the shower glass as I pump into her from behind.

Christ, but I'm close. Watching the way her ass moves, it only takes four pumps before I'm emptying myself inside Cami. Again.

"Fuck, you drive me wild." I kiss the nape of her neck.

She laughs, her breathing still erratic. "I get why married people take honeymoons now."

I snort and nod against her back. "I'll take you anywhere you want to go, Cam."

She turns around and wraps her arms around my neck. "I want to be right here. With you."

"Me too," I admit, kissing her. It's a long, passionate, thorough kiss that centers me in new ways.

With Cami, I'm not go-with-the-flow, Laid-Back Leif, as much as I'm whatever she needs me to be. Her husband.

And I like that more than any other identifier.

We shower together, taking our time and enjoying just being under the hot water. When we're both finished, we dry off with thick towels Mom had the good sense to wash and dry last night.

Then, I pull one of my hockey shirts over my girl's head. She slides on a pair of underwear and combs out her hair. I pull on sweats, and we relocate to the kitchen where I make us pancakes for dinner.

We spend the rest of the night watching TV, talking, and

cracking jokes. Cami's hair dries naturally. I wrap her in a blanket and pull her onto my lap. And I discover what true contentment is.

For the first time in my life, I think I have what my parents share, what my older brothers have found, what Chris has with Casey and Hudson has with Piper. And I get it. I get them.

Because this, with Cami, this is everything.

OVER THE NEXT FEW WEEKS, Cami and I settle into a routine. Into our version of a honeymoon. We go for hikes or runs in the early morning and have smoothie bowls for breakfast.

I kiss my wife good-bye as she heads to work, and meet her and her coworkers one or two times a week for happy hour.

When I head to the stadium for an afternoon, weekend skate, she bakes cookies and spends time sketching. I haven't seen her work yet but the few doodles I've caught in the margins of shopping lists have clued me in—my wife is really talented. She has a true passion and could turn her drawings, her designs, into a career path if it's something she wanted to do.

A few times, we Zoom with my siblings and my parents. My brothers and Annie like Cami instantly. My dad thinks she's good for me. *Grounding* is the word he uses.

Mom is over the moon and as the days stretch into weeks, Mom and Cheryl ramp up their wedding planning.

"You know, before our Crosslake wedding, we have a wedding to attend in Honey Harbor," I tell Cami one night as I flip our burgers on the grill.

She's holding a cup of tea, her feet curled underneath her, as she perches in one of the Adirondack chairs. "That's right! Chris and...Casey?"

"Yep. Their wedding is the last Saturday in July."

"That will be fun!" Cami takes a sip of her tea. "I'll need to buy a new dress."

"Whatever you need. You got the credit card I left you, right?"

She snorts. "You mean the one you slipped into my wallet?"

I shrug.

"I can buy my own clothes, Leif," she says quietly.

I glance at her over my shoulder. "I know you can. It's just...there. In case of an emergency."

She rolls her eyes. "Now you sound like my dad."

"I like your dad," I volley, even though I've only talked to the man once and I don't think he likes me at all. I still have some work to do to get Mr. Coleman and Rhett to welcome me into the family fold. Luckily, Cheryl is putting in a good word for me, and Jenna and I have talked a few times.

Cami sighs. "It's important to me that I can...take care of myself."

I frown, wondering where this is coming from. "Okay. I know you can take care of yourself, and you know you can too. The card is just an extra...insurance. You might see shoes you like."

She laughs and rolls her eyes. "Hey, this Friday, Sam and Tarek want to hit some music festival after happy hour. Maria can't come because her mom has dinner plans, so she doesn't have anyone to watch the baby."

"Oh." I wrinkle my nose. "That's too bad."

"Yeah, but I told them we'd go with them. Is that okay?"

I shrug. "Sure. I'd love to check out more of the local music scene."

Cami grins. "Great! I'll text them to confirm." She pulls her phone out of her pocket and rattles off a text message.

I plate our burgers and turn toward her. "Dinner is served."

"Thank you, kind sir." Cami stands from the chair, and we relocate to the kitchen island to eat our dinner.

And it's easy. Comfortable. Fun.

A lazy summer I never want to end.

SEVENTEEN

Cami

"What's good, man?" Leif exchanges an easy handshake with Tarek as he and Sam enter our house. Sam whistles. "This is a sweet setup, Leif." He points toward the surround sound speakers and big screen television. Leif laughs it off. "It's for all the Hallmark movies Cam watches."

I flip him the middle finger and he pretends to catch it and slip it into his pocket.

Tarek chuckles. "Man, I don't know any married couples like y'all. Thanks for coming with us tonight. There are a few local bands playing, some regional talents, and even a couple of big-time headliners."

"Sounds good," Leif replies, tilting his head toward the kitchen. "You guys want to have a beer before we head out?"

"Sure," Sam says.

As Sam and Tarek follow Leif into the kitchen, my guy tosses me a wink.

"I'll just finish getting ready." I tug on the half of my hair I haven't used my straightener on yet.

"You look gorgeous," Leif replies.

"You have to say that, or you won't get any tonight," I call over my shoulder as I walk toward our bedroom.

"Damn," Tarek mutters.

"Cold-blooded, Cami," Sam hollers. "Calling Leif out like that!"

Leif laughs and I shake my head. But I can't stop my grin. I like that Leif has hit it off with my colleagues. It's important to me that I have my own friends in Knoxville, that I build social connections here that aren't tangled up in his hockey world.

As I resume fixing my hair and makeup in the bathroom mirror, I think about how each passing week with Leif adds more emotional distance between now and the woman I was three years ago.

After Levi broke my heart and left me with the threat of leaked nude photos as well as the possibility of drug-related charges, I lost myself. I forgot how to trust myself fully and became fearful of my own intuition.

My experience with Levi lacks closure and in the months that followed, I flirted and dated and had fun with boys, but I never let them in past the surface. With Leif, I'm starting to open doors I had slammed shut. Granted, he makes it easy. A hell of a lot easier than most men would. The fact that he's my husband is as mind-boggling as it's wonderful. As my confidence comes back, I feel more settled, more grown-up, more like myself, than I have in a long time.

I tuck my hair behind my ears and give myself a once-over. My eyes are bright, my skin glows, and I look happy. Truly content. I smile at myself.

Marriage never looked so damn good.

Flipping off the bathroom light, I head into the kitchen to rally up the boys so we can head to the music festival. Leif insists on driving. I noticed he does that whenever we're getting drinks in a social setting. When I asked him why, he replied instantly.

I never want you in a position where you get in the car with a drunk driver and don't know it. I know my limits and I'll never have more than one when I'm driving you, Cam.

After falling for a guy who pumped me with drugs and chucked a champagne bottle off a seventh-floor balcony, Leif's words were more soothing than he knows.

We enter the music festival and I'm relieved I wore cut-off black denim shorts and a cropped Rolling Stones tee with silver cowgirl boots. I fit in with the overall vibe—laid-back yet edgy.

"Drinks?" Sam asks, taking our orders.

As expected, Leif orders a Coke. He winks at me, letting me know I should indulge, so I ask for a Blue Moon.

Tarek hooks us up with wristbands while Sam grabs drinks.

"You got us the hookup," Leif comments, noticing the VIP stamped on the wristband.

"My sister's dating one of the musicians." Tarek flips his chin toward the stage.

Leif snorts. "Man, that must be rough. Musicians tend to have the same reputations as athletes."

He says it as a joke and while it probably holds some weight, not in my experience. Nope, in my experience Leif is a million times better, sexier, and sweeter than the musicians I used to know.

Sam returns with our drinks, and we head to the VIP section where there are more opportunities to order drinks and food and less people. We cross into the section and grab a corner table that's still available. I slide onto the chair and turn to people watch when my eyes narrow on a guy a handful of tables over.

He's tall and thin, more fit, less lanky than I remember. His hair still sticks up at odd angles. He's got fresh ink on his arms and a few piercings in his ears, one small barbell through his eyebrow. When he turns, his blue eyes—not electric, nothing like Leif's—meet mine. A flicker of recognition flares in his eyes, like he knows me from somewhere but can't place me.

I grip my pint glass and suck in a breath.

You've got to be kidding me.

Levi Rousell stares back, his eyebrows pulling together like I'm a puzzle he's having a hard time solving.

My heart rate doubles, and my hands grow sweaty. My mouth fills with saliva as adrenaline pumps through my veins, causing a bubble of nausea to swell in my stomach.

Leif is facing Sam, talking about something I can't hear, so he doesn't see the panic that washes over my expression. It coats me in a sticky sheen that has nothing to do with the Tennessee temperature and everything to do with the man now standing from his chair and stepping toward me.

Levi strides closer and I sit ramrod straight, trying to get my breathing under control as memories from three years ago flash through my mind like a highlights reel.

Levi kissing me on a Barcelona beach.

Levi pushing me down into the sand and me, gripping at his shoulders, pulling him closer as I gave him my virginity. He still has no idea that he was my first.

Hell, he has no idea who I really am.

Levi and me wandering the cobblestone streets of Grenada late at night. Clubbing until sunrise in Madrid. Waiting for him backstage at a concert where thousands—thousands!—of women screamed his name in Ibiza. And he walked off that stage to my waiting arms and kissed me hard.

Levi wasted and slurring, falling so hard he split his eyebrow and needed stitches. Levi's hold on my arm so tight it became painful. A ring of bruises appeared the following day and he laughed it off.

He laughed everything off. Even me.

And now, he stands in front of me, his eyes clear, his expression thoughtful.

Next to me, Leif turns, his eyes cutting from me to Levi and back again.

"Cam? You okay?" Leif asks.

"I know you from somewhere," Levi announces.

"Holy shit! You're Levi Rousell. From The Burnt Clovers!" Tarek stands and hold out a hand. "I'm a big fan."

"Thanks, man," Levi says, shaking hands with him easily.

He's a completely different man now. I guess rehab really changed him. He used to barely acknowledge his male fans and make a pass at their girlfriends instead. But this version of Levi looks healthy. Happy.

I frown, staring at the guy I used to compare every man I met to and realize that this is my chance. This is my window to get the closure I need. To tell him how badly he fucked shit up for me. And he can't place me? I carried around the mistakes of my time with him for the last three years, allowing them to overshadow everything I did. Every relationship I tried to start. Every decision that required trust in myself.

And he...he doesn't even remember. Not really.

"Knox, what's going on?" Leif's voice is in my ear. His

large hand is on my thigh. Rooting me to this moment. To the present.

"Cami?" Sam echoes.

"Cami," Levi says, understanding dawning in his expression. He snaps his fingers and points at me. "Holy shit. I remember now. We fucked in Barcelona, yeah?"

My heart rate explodes in my temples, blocking out sound. Light fractures. I'm pulled into a vortex of spinning memories and heightened moments.

This is nothing like the blissful time stops I shared with Leif.

No, this is a fucking nightmare.

I open my mouth, but words don't come out.

Instead, I watch as my husband cocks back his arm and launches it at the internationally acclaimed rhythm guitarist of one of the country's hottest rock bands.

Leif catches Levi off guard and Levi's head snaps back.

"Fuck, bro," Levi accuses, whirling on Leif. His eyes are narrowed, his mouth twisted. But he doesn't try to hit him back. Instead, he holds up his hands in a surrender position and again, I'm stuck by this version of Levi. Who the hell is this guy? "That came out the wrong way."

"Cami..." Leif's voice is a whisper in my ear. A thread I cling to. "Are you okay? Talk to me, babe."

I stand on shaky legs. "I gotta... I need to go." I look around, frantically searching for an exit.

And my guy, my husband, is right there. Leif scoops me up and hurries me out of the VIP section. Away from the flailing camera phones. The security. The shouting.

He protects me. He shields me. He brings me to safety.

And I melt into him, even as my body shakes, tears fall, and my two worlds—past and present—collide.

EIGHTEEN

Leif

My thoughts are erratic, my body hopped up on adrenaline, and a new kind of panic I've never experienced before. I place her gently in the passenger seat of my ride and quickly round the truck to slide behind the steering wheel and drive us home.

I need to check on Cami, but I also need to get us out of the parking lot of this music festival, swarming with eyes and cell phones and nosy people.

When we're a few streets away from the mayhem, I pull into a random parking lot and cut the engine. Glancing at my girl, I note how she's tucked herself into a ball, her feet under her body, her forehead pressed against the window.

"Cam," I murmur.

She turns and looks at me. Her eyes are rimmed in heartache, her irises bleeding with regret. "I'm so sorry, Leif."

I shake my head and place a hand on her thigh. I need to

touch her. Feel connected to her. Make sure she knows that I'm here for *her*. "There's nothing to be sorry about."

"You don't know the full story."

"I don't need to. I know *you*."

She closes her eyes and twin tears fall to her cheeks.

Fuck, but it hurts seeing her cry. It twists my chest and burns my throat. It's a different kind of pain too.

"Leif," she whispers.

"Talk to me, babe. I hate seeing you hurt."

She opens her eyes and shakes her head. Her tongue darts out to wet her lips. "That was Levi Rousell. He's a guitarist for The Burnt Clovers."

I nod, my jaw tightening. My molars grind together and my nostrils flare. Yeah, I caught that part. I'd know that fucker anyway because he was splashed across the covers of gossip magazines Annie and her ice-skating friends used to thumb through. One of the girls had a massive crush on him. I know he went to rehab and cleaned up his act and has turned his life around.

"He shouldn't have spoken to you like that," I grind out, furious all over again.

We fucked in Barcelona, yeah?

He said it so damn casually. So cool and clipped. Like he was just remembering the incident. Like he could have had Cami and forgot her.

That pissed me off.

But the fact that he once claimed my wife at all? That made my blood run hotter than lava and my hands curl into fists and my calmness evaporate. I couldn't have held back from hitting him if I tried—and I didn't want to restrain myself. I wanted to knock the fucker out.

I'm even mad at him for holding up his hands in apology.

A part of me wished he lashed out, so I could've dropped him, my reputation be damned.

Cami twists in her seat, facing me straight on. "He was the relationship that ended badly."

Yeah. I got that. "Did you love him?" It's the question I most and least want the answer to. Tension coils lightly in my body as I wait for her response. It doesn't matter that she said they'd only dated briefly.

We got married in a couple of hours.

Feelings are feelings regardless of the time invested.

"I thought I did," she muses. Then sighs heavily. "I fell for Levi fast. He was different than any man I'd ever met."

I feel physically ill. But I lock down my reactions and listen to Cami. I want every word she's willing to give me and none at all. What a mind fuck.

"He was larger than life, you know?" She glances at me and then pales. The tears come faster. "I'm sorry. I'm—"

"No." I shift closer. "No, I want you to tell me."

She exhales and tucks her hair behind her ears. She turns fully and my hand slides off her thigh. She hugs her knees to her chest and presses her back against the passenger door. "I've never told anyone the full story before. I mean, other than my family."

Well, that makes me feel marginally better. That means she trusts me, right? "You can tell me whatever you want, Knox. I'm not here to judge you. I want..." I grip the back of my neck. "I want us to be honest with each other."

She bites her bottom lip. "Levi was this international rock god and I was just...me. A nineteen-year-old kid in Europe for the first time. I studied abroad the first semester of my sophomore year."

"Don't most students go junior year?"

"Yeah," she snorts. "But when I was a sophomore, Jenna

was a senior. I was studying near home, in Minnesota but she went to Pepperdine in California."

I nod, having heard of the university in LA.

"I missed her. And our parents felt better about us being in Europe together. So, I went a year early, she went a year late, and we agreed on Spain."

"That must have been a cool experience for you two," I admit, wondering where I would have gone if I studied abroad. The only thing I did through college was focus on hockey. My brothers were mostly the same. While we're fortunate to have traveled for the game, we never had the exciting adventure of a semester abroad.

"You have no idea how grateful I am that Jenna was with me. I met Levi my first week there. The band was on their European tour and had a handful of dates in Spain. It was... wild." She shakes her head, her eyes flashing. "Being with them, it's like being in another world. It's a level of stardom, of fandom, I can't explain. My sister kept warning me. But I was enamored. At that time, I would have followed Levi to the ends of the Earth."

I work a swallow and drop my hands to my lap as they curl into fists. I hate that Levi fucking Rousell got some of my girl's sparkle. And then he dimmed it.

"He was my first," Cami admits, her voice low. "And because of that, I think I needed to believe that what was between us was real. Even though, logically, it couldn't have been."

I frown. "Don't say that. You—"

"No," she cuts me off. "Don't comfort me. I'm not saying it couldn't have worked because of me. It couldn't have worked because of him. He was so deep into the spiral by then. Drugs, booze, women. Everything was about the party. The moment. And it was fun and reckless and euphoric in this big, exciting way. There was limitless access to all these forbidden things. And I was tempted, curious, excited... I wanted to try everything with him."

Fucking hell. I scrape my upper lip between my teeth. "Did you?" I grate out.

Cami nods. "It all went sour one night. Levi wanted me to take pictures."

I close my eyes, feeling the blood drain from my face.

"I did some lines of coke first. Then, I did everything he asked. I don't even remember passing out. But when I woke up, the hotel room was in a frenzy. His bandmates, personnel, security... It was a nightmare. Levi was put on a plane and entered rehab. I called my sister who called my parents, and we flew back home. And then, it took my parents months—and a lot in legal bills—to acquire those photos so they wouldn't leak and ruin my future."

"Fuck, Cami," I mutter.

She nods. "I know. I fucked up so badly."

"No." I shake my head. "You were a kid who made a bad call. But everything afterwards...it impacted you."

"I forgot how to trust myself. Or lost faith in my ability to navigate things. I spent the next three years drawing inward and letting my mom manage things for me. Then, I realized how much I was missing out on, and I missed parts of the old me."

"Vegas?"

"Embracing the moment," she admits.

I nod. "You regret it?"

"No." Her eyes are serious when they latch onto mine. "I don't have regrets anymore, Leif," she repeats the words to me. "And I will never regret anything with you." She leans forward to take my hand. She runs her fingertips over my knuckles. "Does it hurt?"

I shake my head. "I kind of forgot about it."

Cami snorts. "I can't believe you hit him."

"I can't believe that's all I did."

She glances at me. "I'm sorry for ruining your night."

"I didn't care about the music festival as much as I cared about being with you, Cam. I'm glad you told me the truth. Even though it fucking sucked to hear it."

Her eyes turn wary, and I shake my head to stop her thoughts before they spiral. "I want to know things about your past, Cam. I want to know you."

"I just feel so ashamed," she admits, her voice cracking. "So stupid and naïve. Then, seeing him tonight... There are so many things I wanted to say. There was never any closure, you know? One minute he was there, the next he was in rehab. And it's like what transpired between us never happened. I went home from Spain and Mom became nearly unbearable with her hovering. She was worried I was into drugs. She constantly thought I was lying to her." She smiles softly. "Thank God for Jenna. I can't wait for you to meet her."

"Same," I murmur. I glance through the window behind Cami's head, taking in the random Knoxville backdrop. Yeah, it's a big city but my life here is a simple slice. I may be a hockey player but that's nothing compared to a rock god. There isn't limitless champagne and tours across Europe. What if this isn't enough for her?

What if I'm not enough for her?

When I look at Cami, she's lost in her thoughts again. Her makeup is slightly smeared from her tears, and she looks every bit the scared, naïve, broken-hearted girl I can picture at nineteen.

Never before have I been so fearful of rejection. But I hate wondering if Cami is comparing me to Levi Rousell. I can't fucking stand the thought of not living up to her expectations or the future she envisions.

She never wanted to stay married. I did.

Does she still? Even now, after seeing her first love?

She gave him her damn virginity.

And never got closure.

We sit in silence for a long moment with only the sounds of our breathing. Her phone beeps and when she looks at the screen, she grins.

Is it him? Did he get her number from Sam or Tarek? Is he reaching out?

"Tarek says he and Sam are calling it an early night. He wanted to check that we're good," Cami explains, tapping out a reply.

I don't say anything. I can't.

Because for the first time in my life I'm confused with jealousy, with a possessiveness, I've never felt before. And I hate that too. There are too many complicated feelings—most of them negative—that go against my nature.

"Are you hungry?" Cami asks.

"Sure," I say, putting the truck back in drive. I ease it onto the road and set it in the direction of my house. "What are you in the mood for?"

"Pizza." She shrugs.

"Want to place an order? We can pass by and get it," I reply. I feel like I'm on autopilot, going through the motions. I'm relieved Cami confided in me. I'm thankful that she trusts me enough to tell me her story. But she gave me so much to process.

Is that the incident that has caused her and her mother so much distress?

Is that why she ghosted me after we got married?

Is she still hung up on fucking Levi?

Is she going to disappear on me again?

The thoughts plague me through a sleepless night and throughout the following day.

Even though Cami and I settle back into our routine, something's different. There's an awareness between us now. One where I know the truth of her past and I'm worried, if given the choice, would she choose me for her future?

Would she choose me at all?

NINETEEN

Cami

"Mom and Stella are going to drop into your inbox with a whole slew of wedding items that require your and Leif's approval," my sister tells me on FaceTime.

"Oh gosh, is Mom driving you nuts?"

"And Dad. And Rhett. Her entire life now revolves around your wedding," Jenna shares.

I wince. "Sorry."

"Don't be. It's good to see her excited and invested in something...good for you."

Fair point. "Well, I will admit that it's been nice having the extra help. With Mom and Stella setting the foundation for all the plans, Leif and I have only been consumed with the fun parts."

"And cutting the check," Jenna points out.

I wrinkle my nose. "Yeah. Leif hasn't given any pushback about anything."

"He's a good man."

"The best," I agree honestly.

Jenna smiles softly. "You really are happy."

"I am. I told him about Levi."

"Oh my God, seriously? What did he say?"

"He was super understanding. We actually ran into Levi at a music festival." I recount the story for Jenna. She gasps and sighs at all the right parts and having this conversation with her transports me back to college. Sitting on FaceTime recounting my weekend with my sister—gleaning her reactions, waiting for her advice, just bonding.

"He hit him!" Jenna repeats.

"Without flinching," I confirm. "You should've seen Leif."

"Defending your honor."

"Yeah, I think he really was."

"Damn, Cami. You really are lucky. When you married Leif, I thought you went off the deep end, but you obviously chose him for a real reason. He's the perfect partner for you."

"Thanks, J. I can't wait for you two to meet."

"Me too! I'm going to try to come visit this summer."

I perk up instantly. "Really?"

"Yes! Send me the dates that you'll be away—"

"In Honey Harbor."

"I'm jealous you're going. It looks so cute and quaint. Very romantic." Jenna bats her eyelashes.

"I'm looking forward to it, too." Plus, it will be nice to see Leif's friends again and meet their significant others. I chatted with Hudson's girlfriend, Piper, on the phone and I'm looking forward to hanging out with her during Chris and Casey's wedding weekend. "But I would love for you to come visit. We have a guest room."

"I'm going to try my best with work," Jenna promises. "If

not, you will need to come in early before the wedding anyway."

"True. Hey—did you see the sketches I did?" I emailed them to her a few days ago.

"Yes! And Cami, they're beautiful. You should really consider fashion and design. Especially wedding gowns."

I snort. "I'm working at an accounting firm."

"So? You don't even like it," Jenna reminds me.

"You sound like Izzy." I shake my head. "And it's not that bad."

"You're only saying that because you like your work friends."

I sigh, hating when my sister is right. She's almost always right.

"I'm just saying, your sketches are beautiful. You're talented, sissy."

I roll my eyes, but I'm pleased by her praise. "Thank you, J."

"Think about it!" my sister says enthusiastically.

The front door creaks open and Leif appears.

I smile back at Jenna. "I gotta go. Leif is home from his run."

"Hi, Leif!" Jenna calls.

"What's up, J?" Leif asks, coming into the frame.

I pass him the phone and he and Jenna chat for a few minutes. It makes me happy, seeing two of the most important people in my life, communicate. For the weeks that Levi flipped my world upside down, I don't know if he ever spoke to Jenna. He wasn't interested, he didn't care, and the fact that I couldn't see that for what it was—a giant red flag—shames me.

Ever since I told Leif the truth, I feel lighter. Better. Able to move forward with him without any shadows lurking in the corners of our marriage. It was cleansing and cathartic.

But now, I'm worried about how he's taking it. Leif's been quieter than usual and I think my story caught him off guard. While we're still spending time together, hanging out with his teammates and friends, and making love to each other every night, there's a distance that didn't used to exist.

When I try to talk to him about it, he brushes it off as us still getting to know each other. He gives me the laid-back persona instead of the man behind it and while I want to give him time to process things, I also want the real him. Always.

Leif ends the call with Jenna and passes me my phone. "I hope J can come visit next month."

"Same," I say, following him into the kitchen. "I made pasta for dinner."

"Sounds delicious, baby. I'm starving." Leif walks toward our bedroom. "I'm going to rinse off really quickly."

While he showers, I make us two bowls. Then, we sit at the kitchen island together.

"How was your day?" I like this part of the day best—the part where we confide in each other and exchange stories.

"Beau and Cole are back from Mexico. They can't wait to meet you." He points his fork at me. "Actually, I think you're really going to hit it off with Bea. She's Beau's little sister and Cole's girlfriend. She runs a little art shop downtown—Humble Bee's. She makes pottery."

"Really? That's so cool! I know exactly where you're talking about. I walked through the shop the other day. It's adorable," I gush.

"Yeah. You should talk to her, Cam. I saw one of the sketches you left on the counter."

I blush at his praise. And also, "Which one?"

Leif smirks. "It was a beautiful dress. Bridal, I believe."

My cheeks burn. "I've been on a roll lately with the bridal gowns."

"Oh yeah?" he asks, twisting on his barstool until he captures one of my knees between his.

"Yep," I murmur, grinning back wickedly. "You've given me all sorts of inspiration, you know?"

Leif chuckles and takes another bite of pasta. Then, he slides off the stool and reaches for me. In one quick movement, he tosses me over his shoulder.

"Leif Bang! Put me down!" I cry out, grasping at the back of his shirt.

He smacks my ass lightly. "I'd rather bang you, love."

"Oh, God," I groan at his lame joke.

He tosses me in the middle of our bed and pulls off his T-shirt.

My thoughts spiral and I take a moment to appreciate how gorgeous he is. Perfection.

"Like what you see, Knox?" He slides off his shorts and tosses them in the corner of our bedroom, missing the laundry basket completely.

But I'm checking him out too hard to comment.

His boxer briefs are next to go. His thick cock springs free, already hardening. Already wanting me.

I make a sound in the back of my throat and Leif grins, coming closer.

He leans over me, dropping his fists to either side of my hips. I lean back so I can find his eyes.

"Are you ready to get banged, babe?" he taunts.

"Yes." I surrender, flopping backward and lying like a starfish. "Have your way with me, Leif. Just make it good."

Leif gasps, pausing with his hand on my calf.

"What?" I tilt my head up to look at him.

"It's always good," he says, his expression serious.

I roll my eyes and drop my head back. "It's always fantastic. Stop fishing for compliments, Bang, and get your girl off."

He pulls my jeans clear off my legs. "Like it when you're bossy, Knox."

Leif crawls up my body and I hook my legs over his, keeping him pinned against me. "Promise?" He's the first man I've ever been bossy with. The first guy I've ever let my guard down enough to talk about things in bed. About what I like and what I want. Desires and needs.

Leif brushes my hair back from my face and stares at me. His expression is solemn, his eyes blazing. He studies me as his hand makes another pass over the top of my head. Then he closes the space between us and kisses me hard. "Promise. Like you exactly as you are."

Something settles inside me at his words. I close my eyes, fold Leif into my arms, and give myself to him. He makes love to me slowly. And then again, quick and fast.

And I was right—it's fan-fucking-tastic.

A WEEK GOES by when the first email pops up in my inbox.

The sender?

Levi Rousell.

"No fucking way," I murmur to myself, opening the email.

Hey, Cami—

I hope you don't mind my emailing you. It took me a minute to track down your email—it was on a U of M alumni list—since you don't have any socials. What's up with that?

"You, you dumb fuck," I mutter, narrowing my eyes at the screen. After that night in Spain, I deleted all my social media accounts. I knew how lucky I was to get through that phase of my life without being tagged in a hundred photos, fucked up out of my mind and dropping my face to lines of coke. It was a lesson I didn't want to relearn.

But I digress. Shaking off my anger, I read the rest of Levi's email.

Anyway, since we last saw each other, I've pulled my shit together. Rehab was intense but I've made a lot of amends with a lot of people. Not with you, though. For that, I'm sorry and I'd like the chance to set things right between us. I know that you don't owe me anything but if you'll gift me your time —or let me buy you a cup of coffee just to talk—it would mean a lot to me.

Tell your man he's got a solid jab.

Levi

I sit in silence, rereading Levi's email three times. What the hell am I supposed to do with this? He wants to meet up —to get closure—now?

I heave out a sigh and cross my arms over my chest.

Anger, frustration, and...curiosity swirl though me. I hate that Levi can still affect me, still mess with my head. I also can't stand that a part of me wants to email him back. I want to know what he has to say.

I want closure too.

But why? Why does Levi matter at all when I have Leif? My husband. The best guy. One I can trust and confide in. One who makes me feel whole.

I ex out of the email and close my laptop.

I'm supposed to be confirming wedding plans and now, I can't think straight. I can't think at all because the annoying musician with the messy hair and broken eyes reached out to me. After all this time, he wants to talk. And say what?

It doesn't matter!

Except it does.

I've spent years holding on to anger, on to fear, where Levi is concerned. Wouldn't it be freeing to let it all go? To lay the shit between us to rest? To fully move on, without the shadow of him hovering over me?

My phone beeps with an incoming text.

I grin when I read Harper's name. She's a sweetheart and reached out to me to organize a lunch with her, Bea, Lola, and Maisy. Her text confirms the reservation she placed for today. Unfortunately, Beau Turner's wife, Celine, is currently on location filming a movie. I wonder if she knows Jensen's girlfriend, Bailey.

I push away from the kitchen island and pace around the space. In a short amount of time, my life has changed drastically. In that sense, it echoes my time spent in Spain.

Except this change has been positive, hopeful, and beautiful. I married a wonderful man and we're planning our real wedding. I've made great friends. I love where I'm living and don't mind my work because at the end of the day, I get to come home and sketch. Next week, I'm having a getaway to a quaint cottage town with Leif.

All in all, things are amazing.

I look at my laptop. So, why do I want to email Levi back? Why does his note call to me?

I grip my phone instead and text Harper back.

Then, I leave my laptop behind, shower, and get ready for lunch with the girls.

I force Levi Rousell out of my mind and focus on the life I'm building with Leif.

The life I've always wanted. A future I can believe in with a man I trust.

TWENTY

Leif

I run the pad of my thumb over the pear-shaped diamond.

River Patton whistles between his teeth.

"It's gorgeous, isn't it?" I glance at him.

"Unbelievable," he replies. "With a hefty price tag."

I shrug. I don't care about the price. I want to find the perfect ring. Something unique, something Cami. "I like the pear shape," I tell the jeweler.

He nods and selects a few other options. "Just for comparison," he explains.

"Thanks," I murmur, studying the rings. While Cami's story about Levi Rousell was tough to swallow, I understand now why she was hesitant about giving our marriage a chance. Over the past weeks, we've grown closer but proposing to her, proving that I choose her too, and gifting her a ring as a symbol of my love, will help ease her mind. And when she accepts this token, it will ease my lingering worry too.

The fact that she confided in me about her past with Levi Rousell was a turning point for her. Now, the tradition of this ritual will prove that we're both choosing each other for the right reasons before we marry again in August.

River asks the jeweler a question and he leads River over to a case to look at earrings. River wants to buy Lola and Mia matching sets for Lola's birthday.

I pick up a ring and know it's the one. It's about three carats and outlined with smaller diamonds that drip onto a double band. It's a bit flashy but different, and I think Cami will appreciate that. She likes unique things. I snap a picture and send it to my siblings' group chat.

> Me: What do you think?

> Me: (Image of ring)

Jensen: DAMN, BRO!

King: Wow! She's gonna love it, Leif.

Jake: Did you ask her dad for her hand yet?

I roll my eyes.

> Me: Next on my list.

Tanner: It doesn't really matter what he says. Leif's already married to his daughter.

Jake: It's the point, Mitts. A matter of respect.

Annie: Leif—you did good, big brother! I love it.

Me: Thanks, Annie! That actually means the most—coming from you.

Tanner: Hey!

Jensen: When are you proposing?

Me: Next week, after Chris's wedding.

Annie: In Honey Harbor???

Me: Yes!

Annie: Good job, Leif! This is a fantastic proposal. Everyone else—take notes.

Tanner: (eye roll emoji) Leif's let Cami walk around with a plastic crown ring from a gas station on her finger for the last six weeks. He needs to up his game.

I laugh, but my little brother isn't wrong.

King: Let us know when she says yes!

Tanner: *If* she says yes.

Jake: She's going to say yes, you dumbass.

Tanner: (GIF of a male body builder) She hasn't met the youngest Bang yet.

I chuckle again.

Me: Don't remember you being this funny, Tanner.

Tanner: You should visit me more, Leif.

Me: Count on it.

The jeweler returns.

"This is the one," I tell him.

"An excellent choice, sir," he says, cleaning the ring. He tells me about the diamond and its properties, but deep down, I know this is the right ring, the perfect fit, for Cami.

After River and I make our purchases, we leave the jeweler. Knowing the girls are at lunch and Brawler is taking Mia to her baby music class, we decide to swing by Corks for a beer.

"Look at us." River smirks, shaking his head. "If anyone ever would've told me that the two of us would end up with— hell, even had a chance with women like Lola and Cami—I woulda told them to get fucked."

I laugh. "We've come a long way, Patton."

River taps my knuckles with his. "A hell of a long way."

We drop onto barstools, order some pints and nachos, and hang out.

Right now, my life is exactly as I want it.

I have Cami and that's all I've ever wanted. Her happiness, her love, our future.

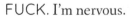

FUCK. I'm nervous.

I stretch my hand several times, as if that will help me work up the courage to dial the number I need to call.

Mr. Coleman.

I managed to get his number from Cheryl, but Cami's

dad and I have yet to speak face-to-face unless Cheryl held the phone up to his face and demanded he say hello.

And now, I've gotta man up and call him. Ask him for his daughter's hand in marriage. Even though, she's legally already my wife.

I close my eyes and drop my head back against the couch cushion. Cami's at work. This is my window.

Just call him!

I dial Hudson instead.

"Hey," he answers on the first ring, and I breathe out a sigh.

Back when I played for the Ottawa Huskies, Hudson and I roomed together in a sweet, two-bedroom apartment near ByWard Market. We confided in each other all the time.

Right now, I need him to weigh in on this.

"Hey," I reply.

"You okay?"

I sigh. "I'm stressed."

"Yeah, I got that." My friend sounds concerned. Man, but Hudson is a good guy. "'Bout what?"

"I gotta call Cami's dad. Ask him if I can marry his daughter," I explain.

At that, he bursts out laughing.

Forget it. I take it back. He's not a good guy at all. "It's not fucking funny."

"I mean, it kind of is," he wheezes. "Leif, you already married her. You guys are living together."

"Fuck," I mutter, squeezing the skin between my eyebrows. "I know. That's why this is so damn difficult."

"I mean, try to see it from his perspective," Hudson points out. "If you married my daughter in Vegas, moved her into your place, and then called me to ask for my blessing, I'd tell you to fuck right off."

"You're not helping."

"I didn't realize you wanted me to lie," my friend points out.

We've always been straight with each other.

"What do you think I should say?" I ask instead.

"The truth. You love her, Leif?"

"Yes," I answer. It's the truth, too. "Look, I know it doesn't make any damn sense but somewhere along the way, between Cami's bright-eyed outlook, her honesty, the damn sketches I find around the kitchen, on napkins and in the corners of grocery lists, I fell in love with her. She's smart and witty. She's adventurous and open-minded. And for the first time in my life, Hudson, I'm not fucking petrified about being rooted. I want it with her—the home and the nights in. I want everything with Cami."

My friend is quiet for a long moment. Then, he says, "Tell him that, Leif. That was honest as hell and he'll appreciate it. Respect you for it. Tell him that."

I exhale and feel the weight of the damn world leave my shoulders. Holy shit. "I love her."

"I know you do. And if you tell her father what you just told me, he'll know it too. I bet that's all he wants for Cami. I think it's what every parent wants for their kid. He wants to know you love and respect her."

"Yeah," I agree. "Yeah, you're right."

"Give him a call now, before you lose your edge," Hudson advises.

I snort. "Thanks, Hud."

"Didn't do a damn thing, man. Call him now and I'll see you next week. Piper can't wait to meet Cami, by the way."

I grin at the thought of our girls hitting it off. Of all of us being together in Honey Harbor. "I'm looking forward to it, too."

"Same. Good luck, Leif."

"Thanks." I end the call and stand from the couch.

I pace around my living room for two laps before I grow a set, pull up the contact info, and call Mr. Coleman.

"Hello?" he answers. His voice is deep and direct, and I automatically know he's the kind of man who exudes authority.

In that sense, he reminds me of my father, which puts me at ease. Men like that want the truth, they want facts, and they don't want to feel like someone is pulling the wool over their eyes.

I should have called him directly when Cami and I first agreed to give things a shot. I should have cleared the air, manned up, and addressed him from the get-go, instead of waiting for Cheryl to smooth things over.

Disappointment coats my tongue and I know exactly what to say.

"Mr. Coleman, it's Leif Bang."

He's silent on the other end but the time is still ticking on my screen, so he hasn't hung up. Yet.

"I'm sorry for not calling you sooner. It was the right move, and I regret not doing it because the truth is, I'm in love with your daughter. And I know how important you and your family are to her. It means a lot to me that we have a good relationship and there's no chance of that without me apologizing to you for not making this phone call weeks ago. And without me telling you how much I love, admire, and respect Cami. I want to propose to her, for real this time, and I want your blessing, sir."

He sighs.

I work a swallow.

"So, Vegas was a mistake?" he asks.

"No." I shake my head even though he can't see me.

"Vegas was the best thing that ever happened to me because I met Cami. Now, do I wish we had done things differently? Yes and no. I love being married to your daughter, but I would have loved for our families to witness our union, which is why I can't wait to marry her again in August."

He clucks in the back of his throat, and I can't tell if he's pleased or pissed by my response. "You've known Cami for under two months, and you love her?"

"Yes, sir."

"Why?" he poses the question.

I bite back my grin because this question? This is easy. "I can't imagine anyone meeting Cami and not falling in love with her," I tell him truthfully. "The biggest blessing here is that she is choosing me, too." Then, I launch into it. I tell him everything I told Hudson and more.

I share about her confiding in me about Levi Rousell, which surprises him. I explain that the trust I have for her is unlike anything I've ever experienced. I admit that being with her has changed me in the best ways possible—for the first time, there's an added sense of responsibility that I was lacking. And I like shouldering it. I want to provide for her, protect her, support her. I conclude with, "I respect her, Mr. Coleman. I love her and I'd like to propose, properly, with your blessing, when we're in Honey Harbor."

Then, I hold my breath. My palms itch and my heartbeat thumps in my temple. Shit, I'm sweating.

Not so laid-back now.

Mr. Coleman is silent again but this time, I get the sense that he's considering all I've shared and choosing his words carefully. "I appreciate the phone call, Leif."

I exhale slowly.

"And I look forward to meeting you in August. I'd like for

us to have a good relationship as well. A part of me wants that for Cami. And a part of me wants that for us."

"Thank you, Mr. Coleman."

"Call me Ben," he advises.

I crack a smile.

"And you have my blessing. I know Cami is truly happy with you. I can hear it in her voice. And the thing I've always wanted for her, Leif, the thing you'll want most in the world if you and Cami have children, is for them to thrive. To be happy. To fall in love. I wish you both nothing less than that." Ben sounds choked up by the end and I'd be lying if I said emotion didn't sweep through me.

Because he was honest. Direct. And sincere.

"Thank you, Ben. I look forward to meeting you, too. If you could do me a favor and not tell Cami, I'd like to surprise her."

He chuckles lightly. "You have my word. That means I won't tell Cheryl either."

I snort. Good call, Ben.

"Best of luck to you, Leif," he continues. "I hope she says yes."

"Yeah, me too."

We end the call and I collapse back onto the couch. Relief flows through me and I laugh to myself.

I did it. It's all good. It's all right.

Then, I text Hudson and my siblings.

> Me: He gave me his blessing. The proposal is on.

TWENTY-ONE

Cami

"This place is magical," I say as Leif and I settle into our bedroom at the massive cottage he rented with his friends for Chris and Casey's wedding. Outside our window, the lake is bathed in moonlight. Pine trees and rich greenery surround the calm lake but in the dark, they look like dancing shadows.

It's quiet. Serene and peaceful.

Romantic.

"It is. I can't believe Chris is from here," Leif remarks, entering our closet where he stored our joint suitcase earlier in the day.

"So is Coach Strauss," I offer, naming the Coyotes Football Coach. "Harper introduced me to him since she works for the team."

Leif snaps his fingers. "That's right. I think he's attending the wedding, too."

Since we arrived this morning, we've spent the day hanging out on the floating dock with Leif's friends. I met Hudson's girlfriend Piper, who I hit it off with immediately. Then, we enjoyed drinks and a wonderful dinner with the bride and groom and their wedding guests.

Tomorrow is the big day, and I can't wait to get dressed up, slip my hand into Leif's, and spend hours dancing in his arms under the stars.

"Yeah." I run my hand over the sweet quilt on the king-sized bed. "If I was from here, I'd never leave."

"I don't think Chris intends to anymore," Leif says, exiting the closet in a pair of sweatpants. "But back in college, he wanted to experience something bigger. This really is a small town."

"It's quaint."

"Sure is," he agrees, kissing me on the lips.

I wrap my arms around his waist and press my ear against his chest. His skin is warm, and I like listening to his heartbeat. Even and steady. Leif hugs me back and we stand like that, enjoying the moment. It's so simple, practically nothing. And yet, it's everything.

I could stand like this all night with my husband. God, it feels amazing to be in love with a man I can count on. Someone I can trust.

"Tonight was fun," I say.

Leif kisses the top of my head. "Tonight was awesome," he agrees. "I'm glad you and Piper clicked."

"She's hilarious!" I pull back, laughing at some of the stories Piper told me about when she and Hudson grew up as neighbors.

"Yeah, I'm happy for Hudson."

"He's happy for you, too," I reply, liking that Piper shared that tidbit of information.

Leif grins and cups my cheek, brushing this thumb along

my cheekbone. "I love you, Cami Coleman. I love being here with you."

I smile, knowing I have hearts in my eyes. Pushing up on my toes, I clasp Leif's shoulders and kiss him hard. "I love you too, Leif Bang," I whisper.

Then, I kiss him slowly. His arms tighten around my frame. We lose ourselves to the moment, to the night, to each other.

And it's more than magic.

THE FOLLOWING MORNING, I wake bright and early. I open the blinds and look out over the glistening lake. "I could get used to this."

"You and me both," Leif replies, coming up behind me and dropping a kiss to my shoulder.

"I can't believe you already went for a run." I wrinkle my nose at him. I was certain I'd wake up before him but, in true Leif fashion, he was already working out by the time I opened my eyes.

He shrugs and pinches my ass. "I was hoping you'd still be in bed."

"I'm sure you were."

Leif grins. "You sure you'll be okay on your own today? I know you hit it off with Piper but—"

"Don't worry about me," I cut him off. "I know you have groomsmen duties to attend to. And honestly? I'm looking forward to enjoying the sunshine and the lake. Maybe even checking out the town."

"Okay." He kisses my cheek. "But call me if you need anything."

"First thing I need is coffee," I admit.

Leif taps my ass. "Hudson already put a fresh pot on the stove."

"No wonder Piper's in love with him," I tease, entering our closet to pull out some clothes.

Leif laughs. "Yeah, I'm sure it's the coffee."

I snort and change into a sundress. Leif rinses off quickly in the shower and when he's dressed, we head downstairs together.

The house is already bustling. Piper, Hudson, James, and Ray huddle around the kitchen table, drinking coffee and eating eggs and pancakes.

"Seriously? I thought I woke up so early!" I tell them.

Ray chuckles. "Not with this crowd." He gestures toward the table. "This crew subscribes to the five AM club."

I wrinkle my nose. "Sounds awful."

"I'm with you, Cam," Piper says, glancing at me. "I woke up about five minutes ago."

Ray laughs. "More like two."

Piper flips him the bird. "Help yourself to some coffee and breakfast," Piper advises, pointing her fork toward the stove.

"Thanks," I say, grabbing a plate. Then, I look at Ray. "You went running too?"

"Five miles," he quips.

"Show-off," Piper mutters.

Hudson, James, and Leif laugh.

Ray scowls.

I fix a plate for Leif and pass it to him.

He kisses me softly. "Thank you, babe."

"Oh, God," Ray moans. "First them"—he gestures toward Piper and Hudson—"and now y'all?" He glares at me and Leif.

I grin. "Can't help myself, Ray. My man's got moves."

The table laughs, even Ray.

"Yeah." He chuckles. "Laid-back Leif definitely has moves. I'm not sure you've seen them all yet, sweet Cami."

His friends laugh again but Leif narrows his eyes, shooting me a look.

I take a bite of my eggs, trying to puzzle out his look. Ray was ribbing him the night we met so I'm not sure why his teasing bothers Leif now.

"Cami," Piper says, polishing off her pancakes. "Want to head into town and do some poking around with me? There are some super cute antique shops and specialty food stores I'd like to check out."

"For sure," I agree eagerly.

"Great!" She stands, taking her plate with her.

I follow suit. "I saw a cute café on the way in yesterday too."

"Crane's Café," Hudson supplies. "You girls will like it there."

Leif tugs on my fingertips. I look down at him.

"You good?" he murmurs quietly.

I nod, dropping a quick kiss to his mouth. "I'm good. I'll see you later."

"The ceremony is at four PM," he reminds me. "I think I'll be busy until then."

I smile. "Have fun."

"You too, Knox," he replies.

"See you guys later," I say, waving to the table.

"Come on, let's get out of here," Piper says, linking my arm with hers and steering me toward her and Hudson's bedroom. "I just need to change but I'll be like, two minutes."

"Take your time," I say.

"Be right back!" Piper slips into her bedroom.

I wander farther down the hall and find a cute sitting area

with beautiful—and fully stocked—bookshelves. I'm about to pull one off the shelf when my phone buzzes in my pocket. It's literally the reason why I bought this sundress—hidden pockets!

I pull it out and frown when I note Levi's name on the screen. Another email. What the hell? My pulse quickens and I suck in a sharp breath.

I should delete it. It doesn't matter what Levi has to say. It doesn't matter anymore. He's in my past and I've put it behind me.

Still, my curiosity rises.

My thumb hovers over the email and before I can fully talk myself out of it, I tap on his message.

Hey, Cami,

I swear I'm not stalking you or anything. I just want to talk. Please, let me apologize for the shit I caused. Let me at least make things right between us. I know it's a selfish ask but I'm asking anyway.

Give me a call when you can and we'll grab a coffee. Then, I won't bother you again.

Talk soon (I hope),

Levi

His number is under his name, and I stare at it. I know for a fact he doesn't give his number out to anyone. It's something he was really selective about back in Spain and I imagine he's only gotten stricter since becoming sober. The last thing he would want is a bunch of people trying to party hitting him up when he's trying to get his life on a new path.

What the hell does it mean? Why is he contacting me?

Is it really to make amends? Or does he still think there's something...there...between us?

No, that doesn't make sense. And it doesn't matter.

It doesn't fucking matter!

I sigh and grip my phone tightly. It buzzes again and I smile when I note Izzy's name on the screen.

> Izzy: Have fun this weekend! I love the photos you sent of your dress! You look hawt, lady, and Leif isn't going to be able to keep his hands off you.

I snort and take a seat in the armchair.

> Me: It's so cute here! I'll send more pictures. What are you up to this weekend?

> Izzy: Going to meet Mia and Tamara for brunch. Then, a hot date tonight! I met him online though so...sharing my location.

> Me: Totally share! Tell the girls I say hello and give them hugs. Call me this week?

> Izzy: Obviously. We'll have to rehash my date.

> Me: I can't wait. xx

I'm about to resume my book perusal when a man's voice rings out. I remain seated instead.

"Man, I've never seen Leif like this," Ray—I think it's Ray —says. I squint, as if that will help me hear better. But I'm fairly certain it's Ray.

"He's happy, bro," James replies.

I freeze, my hands gripping the armrests of the chair.

I glance down at my phone in my lap. Levi's name swims before my eyes. Taunting me.

I slip the phone back into my pocket and pull in a shaky breath.

"Yeah," Ray says, sounding unconvinced. "I just wonder how much of it is real and how much he's trying to convince himself."

What? My heart thrums in my eardrums and I wring my hands.

"What the hell is that supposed to mean?" James asks and I don't miss the clip of anger in his tone. It makes me feel marginally—in the tiniest way possible—better.

"Take it easy," Ray mutters.

"You sound jealous," James tosses back. His sticking up for Leif, for Leif and me, eases my anger slightly.

"Jesus," Ray hisses. "I'm not saying it to be a dick."

A beat of silence passes.

Then, Ray continues. "In all the years you've known Leif, what has he ever failed at?"

"Nothing," James replies instantly. A quick response he didn't have to think about.

"Exactly. Then, he marries a stranger while drunk in Vegas."

"And?"

Ray chuckles. "You know Leif, man. He's been Laid-back Leif since before college, but he's grown up. When he sets his mind on something, does he throw in the towel or double down?"

James is quiet for too long and my doubt grows. Not in a linear fashion but exponentially.

Why isn't James saying anything? Why isn't he sticking up for us?

"Fuck," James says finally.

I sink deeper in the chair and turn my gaze out the

window. Sunlight streams in and the lake beckons. But the magic is gone.

"I don't know, man," James says shakily. "He and Cami seem like a good pair, regardless."

"Maybe," Ray agrees. "But what challenges have they faced?"

"Now, you sound bitter," James points out.

"I'm not saying this because of my shit with Dee," Ray swears. "I'm saying it because Leif is my friend. He doesn't admit defeat; he never has. I don't want him fighting so hard for something that won't last. I don't want it for him, and I don't want it for her. Cami's a sweetheart."

"Yeah, she is," James agrees.

"Hey!" Piper's voice calls out.

"You're still here?" Ray asks. "I thought y'all went downtown."

"Nope, I had to get dressed," Piper answers.

I close my eyes, praying to the universe that none of them discover me sitting here, eavesdropping on their conversation about me.

"Oh, well, have fun," James says, sounding embarrassed.

"Yeah! I just gotta find Cami. Have you seen her?" Piper asks.

A beat of awkward silence passes.

I open my eyes and pull in a breath, pressing my hand against my chest to ease the gallop of my heart.

"Nope. Maybe she's out front, waiting for you?" James suggests.

"Maybe. See you later!" Piper says. I hear her footsteps pad down the hallway.

Shit. Now, I'm stuck here.

"Just keep your thoughts to yourself this weekend," James mutters. "It's Chris's wedding and right now, Leif is happy."

"Yeah," Ray agrees, sounding distracted. "For now."

In the next minute, I hear their footsteps retract and I breathe a little easier. I wait a few more minutes before quietly slipping from the sitting room. I slide into a bathroom and close the door behind me.

Facing myself in the mirror, I suck in a deep breath.

"You're fine. Everything is good. This is right," I remind myself.

But now, I don't feel so sure. With Levi's email burning a hole in my pocket and Ray's words rattling in my mind, self-doubt fills me.

Is Leif trying to prove a point to himself? Does he want this to work because he doesn't want to fail? Or because he's trying too hard to become the man he wants to be—dependable and unshakeable? To me, he already is that guy. But what if he's trying to convince himself? What if he's trying to find reasons to love me?

How can he love me after barely two months together? After what I told him transpired with Levi? And now, Levi is emailing me, and I haven't even shared that news with my husband.

Why haven't I told Leif? Don't I trust him?

A knock sounds on the bathroom door. I jump and flip on the faucet. "Yeah?" I call out, running my wrists under the cool water.

"Cami?" Piper asks.

"Yes! Sorry, I'll be right out."

"No worries! Take your time. I'm ready when you are."

"Okay." But I don't feel light and happy anymore.

Instead, worry consumes me. Skepticism grows. Unworthiness reigns.

Did Leif make a mistake by committing to me? Did I?

I dry my hands on the towel and pull open the bathroom door.

"I'm sorry, Piper," I murmur to the friendly face standing before me. "I'm actually not feeling that well." I press a hand to my stomach.

And it's not even a lie. Right now, I feel nauseous. My stomach twists painfully and anxiety settles like a lump in my chest.

"Oh, no," Piper says, looking genuinely concerned.

Leif has wonderful friends. And they—well, at least Ray —don't think I'm right for him. They've known him for years; I've known him for a fraction of that time. Could Ray be right? Are they all thinking the same things Ray voiced?

"Do you want me to get Leif? They just left!" She steps toward the front door.

"Oh! No, no, don't do that. I don't want him to worry. I'm sure it's just a stomachache." I grimace and hate the next words that come out of my mouth. "Do you mind if I pass on shopping?"

"Not at all!" Piper says, taking my elbow and leading me toward the staircase. "You rest."

I manage a small smile. "Thank you for understanding. If you could avoid mentioning this to any of the guys, I don't want Leif to come back and miss time with Chris. I'm sure I'll feel better in no time."

"No problem. Just remember, the ceremony is at four."

"Got it," I promise, climbing the stairs. "Have fun shopping."

"Get some rest!" Piper says encouragingly.

I nod and make it to the top of the stairs. Then, I enter the bedroom, lock myself in the bathroom, step into the shower, and have a good cry.

It's cathartic. Necessary.

My feelings are all over the place. My thoughts scattered. Am I really letting Ray's assessment throw me for a loop?

Am I really questioning Leif's love for me?

Do I think he's trying to prove a point to himself by staying married?

I think back to our conversation at the bar in Knoxville. Leif's words ring in my head.

I've never done a serious relationship thing—my first attempt can't crash and burn.

Is that still what this is? Or are we past that? Are we truly in love?

Emotionally exhausted, I twist my wet hair in a towel and climb back into bed. I'm relieved when sleep comes, and I take a long nap.

I wake with plenty of time to dress for the wedding, but my head is still a mess. My thoughts unravel in every direction, and I feel sick to my stomach.

Would I feel this way if there wasn't a kernel of truth to Ray's assessment?

Would I feel this way if I had told Leif about Levi's emails?

I pull myself together enough to fix my hair and makeup for the wedding. I dress in a silk, floor-length, cerulean blue dress. I bought it because it reminded me of the color of Leif's eyes.

Right now, even that realization unnerves me.

Am I trying too hard in our marriage? Is he?

I didn't think so but...what the hell do I know? I've never done this before. I've never done anything remotely close to this.

I slide on my strappy sandals and clasp my clutch. I'm relieved the house is still empty so I can head over to the main cottage where the ceremony and reception are being held without anyone intercepting me.

When I arrive, I gasp. The cottage is beautiful. It's decorated in the most gorgeous flowers I've ever seen. The back wall isn't a wall at all but an open space that leads to the lake. Chairs are already set up, an aisle made down the center. People mill about, sipping on flutes of champagne. I spot a few familiar faces, including Coach Strauss. A string quartet plays off to the side. It's almost like stepping back in time—a simpler, more peaceful era.

"Beautiful, isn't it?" a woman next to me asks.

"Gorgeous," I agree. "I've never been here before."

"It's a pretty town," she says.

"Yes. I'm Cami." I hold out my hand.

She shakes it. "Melissa. Are you bride or groom?"

"Um. Groom," I say since Leif is one of Chris's groomsmen. "You?"

"Bride." She smiles. She's beautiful. With dark brown eyes, long black hair, and a perfect smile, she could be on the cover of a magazine. She wrinkles her nose and on her, even that looks cute. "Although the groom is a friend too. I used to date one of his groomsmen." She laughs, as if that time in her life was memorable. Enjoyable.

"Really? Who?" I ask, certain she's going to say Ray.

She bites the corner of her lip as her eyes focus on the dock.

I follow her line of sight and feel my heart leap into my throat.

The groom and groomsmen have taken their places. Chris looks happy and Leif looks...gorgeous. Sexy. Perfect.

It hits me like a punch to the throat.

I'm in love with my husband and he's trying to convince himself to love me back. Otherwise, there's no way he would have stayed with me after I confessed to him about Levi. No man would. In fact, that's probably why he was distant. Why when I tried to talk to him about the space between us, he changed the subject. Part of him pulled away and added distance while the other part is trying to do the right thing.

The committed, dependable, upstanding man thing.

"Leif Bang," the woman beside me breathes.

Shut the fuck up. I inhale sharply, glancing at her. But her gaze is still trained on my husband. My fingers curl into the silk at my sides.

Are you for real today, universe? I look up at the sky. *Because this is getting a little fucking ridiculous.*

I look at Leif and rock back on my heels when I note he's staring right at me. His gaze shifts to my left and then back again, concern crossing his features.

Son of a bitch.

He dated—dated!—the smoke show standing next to me, looking at him like he's her next snack.

I'm not good at relationships. That's what he told me. I wrongly assumed he'd never had one—but did he have one with her?

"There you are!" Piper says, appearing on my left. "Feel better?"

"Much," I croak, feeling like I want to die.

"Great! We better take our seats. The ceremony is about to start." She links her arm with mine and tugs me toward the groom's side.

I turn to look back at the woman, but she's gone, already seated on the bride's side.

I take a seat next to Piper and try to keep my breathing as my mind whirls.

It was Leif's idea to give our marriage a chance. He wanted to try. Why? Because he didn't want to fail.

I wanted to get an annulment or divorce. Why? Because I told him I didn't love him.

And at the time—I didn't. Except now, I do. And this fucking hurts.

Hell, this burns and aches and cuts deeper than any pain I've ever known. Even deeper than when Levi disappeared. This hurts on a level I'm unprepared for and for a second, I can't catch my breath.

The music starts and the bride and her father begin to walk down the aisle. Casey looks stunning. She's glowing, beaming, happy.

I'm supposed to do this next month. I'm supposed to walk down the aisle to Leif and choose him again. My husband.

Except as I sit and listen to Casey and Chris exchange sincere, heartfelt, handwritten vows, I know I messed up.

Leif and I did it all wrong.

Our marriage in Vegas wasn't a spontaneous, adventurous leap of faith.

It was the start of a fucking disaster.

Because I fell in love with him and deep down, I know I'll never be enough. I'll never be worthy.

Leif just doesn't want to tell me the truth. Hell, he doesn't want to admit the truth himself.

So, we're stuck living a goddamn lie. One I fell for.

One I need to cut ties with. But, how?

TWENTY-TWO

Leif

God, she's gorgeous. Breathtaking. Mesmerizing. The most beautiful woman in the room, and that's saying something because Casey is a stunning bride.

I can't wait to see Cami walk down the aisle to me—again —in a month. But this time, our family and friends will be present. I'll finally meet her father and siblings; she'll get to know the Bang brood. It's everything I ever hoped for and today is a little trailer of what's coming soon.

So soon, I can taste it.

The diamond engagement ring sits in my pocket; I've been careful not to stick my hand inside in fear of accidentally pulling it out. Or worse, losing it. To mitigate the risk, I tied a blue ribbon around it. Hudson thinks I'm nuts for carrying it around but I'm scared Cami will accidentally discover it if I leave it behind, tucked into our shared suitcase.

Tomorrow, once the wedding festivities come to a close, and Cami and I are on our way home, I'm going to propose.

Before we leave the town limits of Honey Harbor, I'm going to pull over to a scenic spot I've already scouted. It overlooks the lake. It's surrounded by beautiful, calming greenery. It's quiet and tranquil. A slice of peace in a chaotic world.

That's where I want to propose to my wife.

I want to give her the opposite of what we've already done—chaos in Vegas, calm in Honey Harbor. Two extremes, two experiences, two moments—just us.

This way, we'll have a mini-anniversary, with her purple crown ring and a chapel in Vegas, and a mega-anniversary, with a real diamond and a wedding witnessed by our loved ones. It's the best of both worlds.

Now that the ceremony is over and the bridal party has finished taking the necessary photos, I can finally enjoy a glass of champagne with Cami. I'm glad she had some time to herself today—shopping with Piper, having lunch with the girls. I even saw her chatting with one of Casey's friends, Melissa, who I went on a date or two with years ago.

Cami had looked at me thoughtfully and I wondered what Melissa had said—but it can't be anything bad, we'd parted on good terms, and she knew the score when we started seeing each other. It would just be casual. I'd never done anything real until Cami.

And tomorrow, I'm going to take the next step and propose, since Cami beat me to it the first time. I love that about our story. Hudson and Chris laughed until they cried when I told them that it's my turn to propose. I grin at the memory and my smile widens as I approach her, standing beside the bar.

"You look beautiful," I say, bending down to brush a kiss over her cheek.

She smiles but it doesn't reach her eyes. "Thanks. You clean up pretty well, too."

I frown. "What's wrong?" My hand settles in the center of her back.

She shakes her head, her eyes darting across the venue to Piper and Hudson. "Nothing. Just...felt off all day."

My frown deepens and I tug her closer. She comes easily and places her head against my shoulder, as if the energy just zapped from her body. Damn, I hope she's not coming down with something. "I'm sorry, baby. What can I do?"

Cami shakes her head and pulls away. "Nothing. I'm sure it will pass. Let's enjoy tonight. Let's dance and mingle and have a beautiful time celebrating Casey and Chris. Their love." Her voice hitches at the end.

I study her, wondering if she feels worse than she's letting on. When she threads her fingers with mine, I relent. "Okay, but if you start to feel worse, we can dip out."

Cami blinks fast, as if holding back tears. "I'll be all right." She tips her head toward the bar. "Champagne?"

"Are you sure you should have a drink?"

She snorts. "Trust me, I need one right now."

"Okay," I say, wondering what that's supposed to mean. Before I can ask, Cami places the order and my friends surround us, everyone wanting to toast to Chris and Casey's wedded bliss.

I let out an exhale and decide to talk to Cami about what's bothering her tomorrow. Maybe she really doesn't feel great. Or maybe seeing Casey and Chris marry made her nervous about our wedding. Or maybe I'm just reading into things and all she really wants is to have a great night.

I take a sip of the bubbly.

I can do that. I can give her a beautiful night. A night to remember.

Hell, every night with her is one I'd never want to forget.

WE DANCE every slow song and most fast ones too. I hold Cami close, love the feel of her hand in mine, and sway to the music. I spin and dip her to some other tunes and love how her eyes lighten, bright blue sparkles in her gaze.

She looks at me longingly, like she can't believe this is our life. Most days, I can't believe it either. It seems too good to be true; too easy. No one marries the right person by accident, but I did.

I married the best person on a whim, and I've never been happier.

Hudson cuts in to steal my girl and I laugh as Piper pops up.

"You did good, Leif," Piper says, tucking her dark brown hair behind her ears before taking my hand. "Cami is wonderful."

I begin to dance with her. I didn't know Piper as well as I would if I still lived in Ottawa but since she's almost always around when I FaceTime with Hudson, I know her well enough. Enough that her opinion resonates and I'm happy she clicked with Cami. "She is," I agree.

Piper gives me a long, searching look. Her dark eyes are sharp, studying me with an intensity that doesn't belong in the center of a dance floor at a wedding.

"What's going on, Pipe?" I ask, starting to feel like I'm on the outside of some joke—or a prank—I should be in on. Growing up with as many siblings as I have, you realize when you're missing part of the picture like a sixth sense. The back of my neck prickles and my fingers flex on Piper's slender hand.

Piper sighs. "I've heard a few things today that I think— and worry—may have gotten back to Cami."

"What?" I frown.

Piper chances a glance at Hudson and Cami. Cami's grinning at whatever wild, entertaining story Hudson's recounting. Piper looks back at me, lowers her voice, and whispers, "I heard some of the guys here and some random women as well talking about you. Some say you won't accept failure and that's why you're making this marriage with Cami work. Others are saying you don't do serious and it's only a matter of time until your relationship fizzles. But basically, a lot of people have a lot to say about your marriage with Cami. And if I was her and I heard some of the shit being said, my feelings would be hurt. I'm not telling you this to try to stir the pot; I just want to give you a heads-up. Cami is awesome and I'd hate for her to take any of that bullshit to heart."

I rear back slightly at Piper's words. I've spent the day with Chris and the guys, celebrating my friend's wedding. I think to how Cami said she was feeling off all day. To how she looked upset earlier. Am I missing the signs? Did someone say something to her? Is she...worried?

"Thanks for letting me know, Piper," I say, squeezing her hand. "I appreciate that."

She nods. "I know, Leif. And trust me, I'm not one for gossip. But I know firsthand how misunderstandings can ruin a good thing." Her eyes find Hudson again and I'm sure she's recalling her history with him. The years they lost—years of friendship and trust and support—due to a lapse in communication.

The song ends, I thank Piper for the dance, and I find my girl.

She's waiting for me, another champagne flute in hand.

"How are you feeling, Knox?" I ask, my hand slipping around her waist. Right now, I want her close. I wish I could tell her how much she means to me, how none of the shit circulating this weekend applies to her, or us. But this isn't the right time for the conversation we need to have.

Besides, what help would words do when actions will prove stronger? Tomorrow, I'm going to propose, and she'll know—with certainty—how deep and true my feelings for her run.

"Better," she says, a soft smile on her lips. But she still holds herself apart. For the remainder of the night, there's a distance between us that wasn't there this morning.

I'm not sure I'd pick up on it without Piper's warning but now, it's obvious. And I hate it. When the wedding is over and I take Cami back to our room, she slips off her dress and comes to me.

God, but she's beautiful. She kisses me deeply, her arms encircling my neck. I dip her, bending my body over hers as I try to show her my love. We come together desperately, as if we both have something to prove. I suppose we do.

When Cami pushes me onto the bed and straddles my hips, I grab her ass and squeeze. She smirks, her eyes flashing. Half sorrow, half fire. I can't get a read on her but I'm along for the ride. I'm here for whatever she needs tonight.

And tomorrow, tomorrow is for talking.

She presses on my shoulders until I flop back and she hovers over me. "What do you want, Leif?"

"You," I tell her truthfully.

Her chest rises and falls and her eyes bore into mine. "Why?"

Fuck, but I hate how her voice cracks.

I grip the back of her thigh, sliding my palm up and down the stretch of skin from her knee to her ass cheek and back again. "Because I love you, Cami."

She shakes her head. "But why, Leif?"

Her insistence is bewildering. I move to sit up so we can

talk right now. To hell waiting for tomorrow. If she needs the words, the ring, I'm ready to give it to her.

"No." She shakes her head and pushes me back into the mattress. "I don't want to talk," she admits. "Not when we can do this instead." Then she presses her mouth to mine and her body rolls over me.

With the bubbly and tequila shots I took with the guys buzzing in my head, I succumb to her lead. And fuck, it's hot.

Cami grinds against me, my cock already hard and needy. Her full breasts are heavy as they swing above me and it's all I can do but shift up and draw one into my mouth.

She sighs contently as I lap and suck at her sweet nipple. Her hand fists my cock and I nearly see stars. "Cami."

"Want you, Leif. Right now, I fucking want you," she pants.

It's edgy. It's reckless. It's heady and desperate and fuck, I want her too.

Cami guides me to her opening and slowly works her way down, taking each inch of me until she bottoms out and I swear. My hands grip the tops of her thighs as she settles over me.

Her hands are on her own body now. Kneading her breasts, pinching her nipples. It's the hottest fucking show of my life and all I want to do is watch her take. I want to watch her move and hear her groans and witness her fall over the edge.

She sets a pace that has me thinking of every fucked-up thing imaginable to hold on until she releases. And she chases her orgasm, moving her hips, shaking her ass, bouncing up and down, until her mouth drops open and she cries out my name.

As soon as she orgasms, she falls forward, collapsing on my chest. I hold her against my body as I thrust up into her. I feel ready to explode. My cock pulses in her pussy and my blood thunders in my eardrums. I'm half out of my mind with lust, with need. Spinning out of control and unable to think clearly.

On the fourth pump, I bite out her name. "Fuck, Camille." I come inside her on a roar.

We stay like that, sated and spent, for a long time. At some point, my breathing regulates and my ability to think comes back. I exhale and tighten my hold on Cami.

Wetness coats my forearm and I frown, giving her a little shake. "Cami?"

She shakes her head but doesn't reply.

Fuck. Is she crying? Panic rises inside and I shake her harder. "Hey. Knox, what's going on?"

"Nothing," she sniffles, sliding off me. She moves toward the bathroom, and I follow, nearly passing out as the blood rushes to my fucking head.

Hell, tonight is a head trip. Highs and lows and I've got no clue which way is up.

"Baby, what's wrong?" I enter the bathroom behind her.

She cleans up quickly. Her face is splotchy when she looks at me.

And my heart fucking breaks. My girl is straight up crying.

"Talk to me," I demand, my panic rising. What is going on? What am I missing?

"Oh, Leif," she says, wrapping her arms around my waist.

She hugs me hard and I hold her.

"Leif, let's go to sleep."

"What?" I frown. "No. Let's talk."

"Tomorrow," Cami whispers. "Please, I'm exhausted and emotional and... Tomorrow."

"Baby, are you okay? Did something happen? I need you

to give me something." No way can I sleep with her crying beside me. Not until I know what's wrong. Not until I know how to fix it.

"I'm okay. Today was just...a lot. Now, I'm tired and emotional and a little bit tipsy. Plus, that was intense." She gestures toward the bed. "Let's sleep, okay?" She takes my hand and tugs me toward the bedroom.

"Okay, baby." I kiss the top of her head. "I'm just going to shower quickly."

She nods and returns to bed. I rinse off, trying to collect my thoughts.

I think over the details of the day. I'm grateful for Piper's heads-up but I still can't pinpoint what happened. What am I missing? Where did things go awry?

I towel off and pull on a pair of boxers to sleep in. When I slide into bed, Cami is already asleep. Her face is peaceful in slumber, her lips pursed into a delicate pout, her eyelashes dark against her cheeks.

God, but I fucking love her. Whatever happened today, I'll fix it. I'll make everything better tomorrow.

The thought settles me some. I wrap my arm around Cami, pull her into my chest, and hold her close. Then, I follow her into sleep.

When I wake in the morning, her side of the bed is empty.

"Cami?" I sit up, looking around the room. My heart rate picks up instantly, as if warning me of danger. I stumble from the bed and glance around the room. Our suitcase is still in the closet, but something feels different.

Off.

Did she head out for a coffee or a walk?

Her phone is gone. So is her purse.

What the hell? I check the time and note it's after eleven AM.

When did she leave? Where did she go?

I race into the bathroom and note that her makeup bag, her hairbrush, her fucking toothbrush are all gone.

Is she coming back? Is she done?

Is she ghosting me? Again.

Déjà vu rocks through me and I stumble, reaching out to grab the doorframe. Nausea rolls in my gut, making me light-headed and shaky.

Cami left me. On the day I was going to propose, she fucking disappears. She doesn't want what I want. She never did.

Hell, she told me as much.

I want to start my life. On my own terms. Not as someone's wife. But as me, Cami Coleman.

Did I force the issue? I think back to deciding she'd move in with me, to roping her into my life, into meeting my friends, to insisting that I hang out with hers. I thought we were merging our lives together. I thought we were moving forward.

Was I off base on everything? Was I fighting a losing battle from the start?

I call her but as expected, it goes to voicemail.

> Me: Cami, please let me know you're okay.

> Me: We need to talk.

> Me: I don't understand. Please, call me.

Fuck. I look at the empty bedroom, feeling like dropping to my knees and fucking wailing.

Instead, I force myself to pick up the room. To dress for

the day. To check that the blue ribbon attached to my fucking dream is still tucked into my pocket.

The house is quiet as I pad downstairs for a cup of coffee. Out the back windows, I see my friends gathered on the floating dock. They're drinking beers and cocktails, taking the kayaks and stand-up paddle boards for a ride.

I need to get the fuck out of here.

I don't want to admit the truth to my friends. Not until I know what the truth is. As quickly as possible, I dash up the stairs, zip up my suitcase, stow it in my rental, and leave the house behind.

When I get to the scenic spot where I planned to propose, I pull over. My heart is in my throat, my head pounds, and I feel positively ill.

I rattle off a text to Hudson, letting him know we had to leave, and I'd touch base with him later.

Then, I text Cami again.

> Me: Knox, how did you get home?

> Me: I have the car.

> Me: Did you Uber to the airport?

> Me: Are you okay?

> Me: Please, just call me.

I look out over the beautiful lake. The serene tranquility. It mocks me and I flip it the finger. A giant fuck you to this slice of peace. What the hell was I thinking? I'll never have this.

The one relationship I tried—my fucking marriage—is crashing and burning and I don't even know why.

I pull back onto the road and drive to the airport. I'm hours early for my flight, which wasn't scheduled until tonight. Which flight did Cami take? Is she already back in Knoxville?

Two hours later, my stomach grumbles. I post up at a bar in the airport and order a burger, even though I don't feel like eating. Sliding onto a barstool, I tug out my phone.

And all the pieces click together.

"Son of a bitch," I mutter, staring at the screen.

> Hudson: You okay, man? Where are you?

> Hudson: What the fuck is going on?

> Hudson: (Image)

It's Cami having a coffee—at the fucking Coffee Grid in Knoxville—with Levi Rousell.

I'm sitting here, going out of my mind with worry, and my girl—my fucking wife—is on a coffee date with another man. With the goddamn rhythm guitarist for The Burnt Clovers. With a guy whose fame is so damn huge, he can't even get a fucking coffee without someone snapping a photo.

Fuck this.

I tried. I gave her the best of myself and she...she still fucking chose him. A man who nearly ruined her life. A man who left her in a time of need. A man who barely remembered the fact that he once had her.

Disgust twists my stomach and I drop some bills on the bar, unable to touch my burger. I rush to the bathroom and drop to my knees in front of the toilet, vomiting the cocktails I consumed last night.

A sticky sheen coats my skin and I feel hollow. Bereft. Fucking empty.

I grip my phone and send Cami one final message along with the photo of her and Levi.

Me: (Image)

Me: I'm done. It's over. My lawyer will contact you soon.

Then, I power off my phone, toss it into my bag, and stew in my thoughts until it's time to fly back to Knoxville.

But now, it no longer feels like home.

TWENTY-THREE

Cami

My head is all over the place.

What the hell am I doing?

Slipping away from Leif, from Honey Harbor, before the sun rose was a gut instinct. A knee-jerk reaction. A whirlwind.

And I'm supposed to be past those.

Leif is stability. He's safe. He's...home.

But I don't deserve it. I don't deserve him. I'm elated one moment, doubting myself the next, and uncertain where I fit. I'm a fucking train wreck. How can I allow a man like that—a man as good and whole and loving as Leif Bang—to commit to me again, in front of our family and friends, when I've doubted him, doubted us, from the very beginning?

He doesn't fail. He doesn't quit.

I do.

The way he smiled at me during the wedding, the praise that fell from his delectable mouth, the consideration he showed, making sure I finished before he found his release, he's a good man.

And I'm a mess. I don't know if I've ever *not* been a mess. I'm the girl who lives life on the edge. The woman who walks in a rainstorm and gets a tattoo because it feels right in the moment. I'm the woman a guy marries by mistake in Vegas. I'm not the one he commits his life to afterwards.

The sooner Leif realizes that, the better.

"Thank you," I tell the Uber driver as he pulls in front of Leif's home. I caught an early flight back to Knoxville. I have a handful of hours to pack up some clothes and figure out my next play.

I've spent the entire flight debating where to go.

Maria would take me in in a heartbeat, but she has a routine, a baby, and I don't want to throw a wrench in her carefully planned schedule.

Tarek and Sam would both loan me their couches but my tears, my scattered thoughts, would cause them to worry.

Harper Henderson, Damien's fiancée, is another option but I don't want to alert Leif's teammates to my spiral and shame. What he chooses to share with his team, with his friends, is his business. I shouldn't take that choice away from him by appearing on any of their doorsteps and ugly crying.

That takes Maisy, Lola, and Bea out of the running as well.

I scurry into the house, pack a suitcase with necessities and some clothes, and grab another Uber.

Then, I call my brother.

"Cam?" He answers on the first ring, the way he always does when I call. Except I haven't called recently because I didn't want to face his ire, his hurt, that I would marry a stranger in Vegas and not tell him.

Although Jenna has mediated between us, and Mom's

approval of Leif has gotten Dad and Rhett on board, right now, I need my brother's council. Jenna provides emotional support. Rhett springs into action.

"Rhett," I say, tears forming a lump in my throat.

"What the fuck did he do?" my brother demands, reading my voice correctly. I'm hurt. But it's a pain of my own making.

"I messed up," I admit.

"What happened?" He gentles his tone. "Did he hurt you?"

"No, it's worse. I hurt him."

Rhett is silent for a long beat. Then, "What do you need, Cami?"

"I don't know where to go. I don't know what to do," I say, before spilling the entire story of our time in Honey Harbor. About his friends' reservations, the smoke show he dated, the solid group Leif keeps company with. "They're the real deal, Rhett. Leif is the real deal."

"So are you, Cam," Rhett reminds me.

I snort. Drag my forearm across my face. "You have to say that; you're my brother. But I can't let him tie himself down to me. He's trying to make this work and it's a lost cause. *I'm* a lost cause."

"Don't talk about yourself like that," Rhett growls.

"Levi messaged me."

"Fuck," my brother growls.

"And I didn't tell Leif. I didn't tell him even though Levi's reached out twice. To make amends."

"Fuck him and his amends."

I stifle a chuckle. My brother can't stand Levi Rousell.

"Where are you, Cam?" Rhett asks.

"Driving around in an Uber wondering where to go," I admit.

My brother snorts. "Sit tight. I'll call you back in five." He disconnects the phone.

The Uber driver meets my eyes in the rearview mirror and gives me a soft smile. "If you love him, he'll understand," he offers.

"I don't deserve him," I try to explain.

He shakes his head, his eyes crinkling at the corners. "Love doesn't pick and choose. Love just loves."

My phone rings again, and I answer. "Rhett."

"There's a room reservation for you at a hotel downtown. I'm texting you the details. You have three days, Cam. Three days to figure this out. If you haven't made a plan by then, I'm coming to Knoxville."

"Rhett, I'm sorry."

"Don't be sorry. Be honest. What do you want, Cam? You can't keep shrinking yourself, or your life, because you're trying to live up to someone else's expectations, or you're scared, or you don't feel worthy enough. That's a cop-out and you used your pass three years ago. Now, it's time to woman up. If you want to make your marriage work, do it. And if you don't, give Leif a divorce and let him move on. But only because you don't want to be with him, and you don't want to put in the effort to try. Not because you're making excuses."

I sniffle as my brother drops some hard truths on my head. "I never thought you'd defend Leif."

"Me neither," Rhett admits. "But he sounds like a good guy."

"The best."

"Figure out your shit, Cam."

"Thank you, Rhett."

"I love you, Cami. I bet Leif does too. Maybe you should try being open to that. Text me when you get to the hotel."

"I will," I promise.

Rhett and I hang up and I tell the driver where to go.

Thirty minutes later, I'm settled into a simple, clean hotel room in Knoxville. It's lonely and centering at the same time.

I miss Leif. I miss Honey Harbor.

But can I truly make him happy? Can we make our future bright and beautiful?

I don't want to "make it work." I want it to *soar*.

You can't keep shrinking yourself, or your life, because you're trying to live up to someone else's expectations, or you're scared, or you don't feel worthy enough. That's a cop-out...

With Rhett's words ringing in my head, I take a shower. I dress in fresh clothes. I sling my purse across my body and decide to take a walk. Get some sunshine. I head to the Coffee Grid for a fresh latte.

I just sat down at a table in the back when a guy slips into the chair across from mine. I look up, about to tell him the table is already taken. I suck in a sharp breath instead.

"I'm not stalking you," Levi Rousell promises. His hair is a mess, and his eyes are clearer than I've ever seen them. "You being here at the same time as me is kismet. Fate." He snorts. "If you believe in those types of things."

His words land like a kick to the breastplate.

I do. I believe in destiny.

I believe in chance encounters because it gifted me Leif.

But right now, I can take this moment and say my piece. Get the closure that has alluded me for years.

I sit up straighter and level Levi with a look. "I got your emails."

"You didn't answer."

"I wasn't sure what I wanted to say," I admit.

He snorts. It's that same cavalier response I remember from Spain. When he didn't have any worries—not a care in the world. When the future was tinged in possibility that stretched larger than what I could comprehend. Levi had the world at his fingertips, and he tossed a lot of it away. Not all of it, but a lot. "Do you need more time?" he jokes. "I can take a walk around the block and circle back."

"Nah." I shake my head. "I know what I want to say." Then, I frown. "Why are you even here? The music festival is over."

"My sponsor is from here. He opened a rehab facility with the support of the Harrison Foundation. I connected with a few people and check in a few times a year."

"Oh, well, that's respectable of you."

Levi's grin widens. "I'm sorry I didn't recognize you at first. But now that I have, I can't believe I could have ever forgotten you, Cami Coleman."

I arch an eyebrow. "Except you did. You dropped me so quickly and it fucked with my head in ways you'll never understand." I take a cleansing breath. "I never had sex before you, Levi."

His eyes widen and shock coats his expression.

"I never tried drugs before you either," I continue.

He winces, looking ashamed.

"I never took naked photos or tried so fucking hard to get someone, a man, to want me. To like me. To see me. And the worst part is, it wasn't because you were a rock god." I chuckle. "I mean, sure that was appealing at first. But the more time we spent together, the more I got glimpses of you as a person. Your outlook. Your music. Your passion. I liked that you had these deep friendships with your bandmates. I loved watching you perform and seeing the crowd accept you. I thought it was brave. I mean, how vulnerable to put yourself out there in the ways you did. And I thought you saw me too. But you didn't; not once. And when you nearly overdosed and I got dragged out of a hotel room, half incoherent and practically naked, I hit a type of rock bottom I didn't know existed. I lost the ability to trust my instincts. Fuck, I lost the ability to trust men in a way that counts. In a way that's not surface level. And instead of being fucking smart, I got scared. I made my world smaller. I let my mom take over managing parts of it. The weeks I spent with you, and the heartache that followed, made me lonely yet desperate to connect. And that's not all on you—I know that. It's on me. But I couldn't reconcile my complicated feelings for you and what a healthy relationship is supposed to be. And then, I met a man in Vegas and asked him to marry me." I smile at the thought of Leif. "And he is lightyears out of my reach. I don't deserve him and I'm fucking terrified I'll break him. Let him down. Hurt him. But he sees me, Levi. He sees me and loves me anyway and I don't know what the fuck to do with that." I toss a hand in his direction. "I don't know why I'm telling you this."

"Because you have no one else to tell," he murmurs.

I narrow my eyes at him.

He shifts in his chair, studying me. "And you know I won't judge you. You can't name a mistake I haven't already made. It's the guy who hit me, right? That's your man?"

I nod, rolling my lips together.

"I deserved the punch," Levi remarks. "What I said to you—it came out wrong. But I deserved the hit anyway."

I nod. He really did.

"And you deserve a man like that, Cami Coleman. You are deserving of a big love and a partner who really, truly *sees* you. I am, too. Just because we fuck up doesn't mean we can't get better. It doesn't rule us out of ever having happiness or trust or commitment. I had no fucking clue that I was your first and I'll carry that with me. I'm sorry. Genuinely fucking sorry that I played any role in you feeling like you can't trust the woman you are." He looks at me, his eyes tracking over the planes of my face. His sincerity oozes from his pores and I know he means it. He really wants to make amends.

His words knock a weight off my shoulders. I didn't think hearing them would matter as much as they do. "Thank you," I say.

Levi nods. Drags a hand through his hair, making it stand up in random directions. "But you do trust yourself, Cami."

I lift an eyebrow.

He smirks. "On some level, you do. Or you wouldn't have chosen your husband as your random proposal. There's a reason you picked him. And there's a reason you haven't thrown in the towel yet. Hell, you're still married to the guy."

Tears prick my eyes as I think of Leif waking up alone, abandoned, in Honey Harbor after the night we shared. I blink them back.

"What if I'm not good enough for him?" I whisper.

"If you weren't, that question would never enter your mind," Levi replies.

Surprise rocks into me at his observation.

"If you weren't the right woman for him, you wouldn't care about hurting him. You wouldn't overthink being enough. You'd just take. That's not you, Cami. And anyone who really, truly sees you, sees that." Levi takes a sip of his coffee and raises his eyebrows, as if daring me to challenge his point.

I don't. Because what he said resonates.

I do care about Leif. Fuck, I love him.

And the only way to be worthy enough is to be worthy enough.

Not leave him behind in Honey Harbor and hide out in Knoxville.

It's to show him. It's to commit. It's to fully step into the role of being his partner, his teammate, his wife.

"Anything else you want to say?" Levi asks.

"I liked your last album," I admit.

Levi laughs. It's uninhibited and honest. It makes me smile.

He taps the tabletop with his palm. "The next time you and your husband roll through Boston, let me know. We'll connect."

"Okay," I say.

Levi stands from the table and holds out his arms. I stand and give him a hug. And it's the closure I needed. It's full circle. Who would have thought Levi Rousell would have helped me find mental clarity? After all this time.

"Thanks, Levi."

"Thank you, Cami. I'm glad I had the opportunity to make things right between us."

"You headed home?" I ask.

"Heading to the airport now. This was just a detour." He lifts his to-go coffee cup.

I snort. "Kismet."

He nods. "Take care of yourself."

"You too." I sit back down and watch as he walks out of the Coffee Grid.

I sit for a long time and take even, deep breaths. I put my past to bed and feel like I can finally look to the future.

Reaching into my purse, I power on my phone. I need to call Leif. I need to apologize. I need to make fucking amends.

But when his stream of text messages appears on my screen, my heart leaps into my throat and panic rushes through my limbs.

Tennessee: I'm done. It's over. My lawyer
will contact you soon.

I grip my phone tightly and focus on breathing.
Leif has every right to be angry, but we're not done.
Hell no. For us, this is just the beginning.
And now, it's my turn to convince him.

TWENTY-FOUR

Leif

For two days, I stew in silence.

My house feels fucking strange without Cami's presence. I miss her silly bath bombs and the robe that used to hang on the hook on the back of the bathroom door. I miss the scent of her perfume and even finding strands of her hair stuck to my T-shirts when I pull them from the drier.

Hell, I miss my wife.

Damien's called. Jensen and King. Even Annie.

Dad's texted. Mom's left an alarming number of voice notes.

I've told everyone that I need a few days to myself.

Because of course, they saw the photos of Cami and Levi having coffee. Everyone in the fucking country has seen them and I'm the poor bastard whose wife dumped him for a rock god.

That cuts on a different level. Knowing that Cami left me in Honey Harbor to have a fucking latte with a man who left her drugged in a hotel room is a hit my ego can't take.

And it hurts. It hurts to know I'm going to get a divorce. That I couldn't make my marriage work. That I couldn't convince Cami that we're amazing together.

Because we are.

She made me feel rooted in a way no one has. She made the future I yearn for feel tangible. We changed my house into our home and with her, events—like weddings and time with friends—took on new meanings.

The pride I felt watching her connect with my team-mates, the genuine joy of her clicking with Piper, the delight I felt when my friends told me she's the one. Did I read it wrong? Did they lie?

How could she do this to me again? And how could I not properly see the signs?

Am I that desperate for what my parents have? For what Chris and Hudson have found with Casey and Piper? For what my brothers have discovered with their women?

I'm still carrying around Cami's engagement ring but now, instead of a source of hope, it's a reminder of my own delusions. She never wanted to be my wife. She never wanted what I yearned for.

I'm the fool who thought I could change her mind.

Since I returned to Knoxville, Cami's sent me text messages and voice notes. I've sent her calls to voicemail. I'm not ready to face her. I'm sure she wants to arrange a time to come and move the rest of her belongings out of our house. She grabbed a bunch of her clothes, but not all.

And when that day comes, the loneliness will hit harder. Weigh heavier. I'm not ready to face it and as a result, I'm ignoring her along with everyone else.

I spend the day playing video games. Since I'm ignoring

reality, Jensen and Bailey make it a point to connect with me through Realm Crusaders and I spent hours gaming with @PhantomKnight and @EmpressHollywood.

After they sign off, I follow suit and force myself to eat dinner. To shower. To meander around my house wondering how I'm going to face my family and team. What do I even say?

I left my lawyer a voicemail but ignored him when he called back. I'm not ready to give up. And the worst part is, it's because I love her. I want Cami. I miss her so fucking much.

I'd rather fail at every other aspect of my life than give up on us. Not because I can't admit defeat but because my life doesn't make sense without her. I don't care about proving a point as much as I want to just love on my wife.

My phone rings and I silence it when I note Hudson's name.

A minute later, a text comes through.

Hudson: Pick up your phone.

Hudson: I'm not joking.

Hudson: I'll keep calling.

Hudson: And texting.

Hudson: And—

I dial him.

"I knew I'd get through eventually," he answers.

"You're annoying as fuck. I don't know how Piper puts up with you."

Hudson laughs. "Good. You're making jokes."

I sigh and take a seat on the couch. Leaning back, I stare at the ceiling.

"How are you, man?" Hudson asks.

"Terrible," I admit, pathetically. "I miss her. I miss her so damn much and I fucking hate that I'm this gutted about something I knew from the start."

"You didn't know this from the jump. I saw Cami with you in Honey Harbor. She loves you, man."

"Or she's a fantastic actress," I counter. I should ask Bailey.

"You can't fake love," Hudson disagrees.

"Then what went wrong?" I sit up, frustrated. "What the hell did I miss? Piper told me there was some chatter at the wedding, but I don't think that would give Cami cold feet. And even if she had doubts, wouldn't she talk to me?" I think back to our last night together. She was definitely upset.

God, I wish I pressed her to talk in the moment. Why did I put it off to the next day? The next day, she was gone, and I was fucking alone.

"Maybe she just had to work some things out," Hudson says slowly. "She messaged Piper."

I stand from the couch and begin to pace around my house. "She did? Why? What did she say?"

"That you haven't listened to any of her messages."

"How do you know that?"

"She told Piper if you had, you would have called her back by now."

I swear colorfully. Hudson chuckles.

"Man," he says, "give your girl a call. You two have to sit down and talk like adults. Like married people. The problem here isn't that one of you doesn't care. The issue is that you both care too much. Sit down, talk, listen, discuss. 'Cause right now, you're both hurting. And the only way forward is through it."

"When the hell did you start doling out relationship advice?" I argue.

"I lost years of having Piper in my life because I was an idiot," Hudson reminds me. "I learn from my mistakes, Leif. Do you?"

I curse at him. He laughs again.

"Marrying Cami wasn't a mistake," he says. "But not giving her your vows in ten days? That will be. Call your wife." Then, he fucking hangs up.

I glare at the phone, feeling more agitated than before Hudson called. See? This is why I was ignoring everyone. It's better that way. I'm too angry and depressed to have a rational conversation.

A knock sounds at the door and I glare at the ceiling, at the fucking powers that be. "Seriously?" I ask.

The doorbell rings.

Heaving out a sigh, I stride toward the door and rip it open, about to shoot down the unsuspecting canvasser or salesperson on the other side. Instead, my ire dies in my throat.

"Cami," I mutter. "What are you doing here?"

She stands on the front porch, her body tight with tension. She rocks forward on her toes, then back on her heels. She's biting her bottom lip, worried. She pushes her bangs out of her eyes and looks up at me with pure heartache in her expression.

She looks paler than I've ever seen her. Her eyes are rimmed red, and her face is bare. Beautiful but sad.

And fuck I don't ever want to see her sad.

"I need to talk to you, Leif." Even her voice sounds raw.

I can't help myself. I'd rather feel gutted than see her in

pain. I hate the remorse in her expression. Can't stand the guilt in her tone.

I open my arms and she falls into them.

The second she's enveloped in my embrace, I can breathe for the first time in days. I hold her close, feel her warmth, breathe in her scent, and know she's it for me.

Whether she chooses me or not doesn't matter; I'll never love another woman the way I love Cami.

"Can I come in?" she whispers.

"Of course you can, Knox." I step back so she can enter the house.

But fuck it's going to kill me if she's just here to pack up and go.

She walks to the kitchen island and places down an envelope.

I frown. Did Cami get her own divorce papers drawn up? Hell, is she here to fucking serve me?

"I saw Levi," she says.

"I know," I reply, crossing my arms over my chest. God, I hope she doesn't tell me about him. I couldn't fucking stand it.

"It was by chance. I ran into him at the Coffee Grid."

"Sure," I mutter.

"I'm serious, Leif." She wrings her hands together.

I swear and grip the back of my neck. "All right," I agree, wanting to believe her. She seems sincere about it.

"I got...closure," she murmurs.

"Good for you." I mean it, too. The last thing I want is for her to go through life hung up on a guy who broke her heart in college.

"And I talked to my brother," she continues.

Great. I'm sure Rhett Coleman sang my praises. I walk

closer to Cami, wondering where she's going with this. What is her point?

"I spent the past few days thinking," she says, pulling a paper out of the folder. She holds it up. "This is our marriage certificate. I took it from the bedroom."

I read the words and nod my confirmation. It's the same paper I had stored in my nightstand after I got home from Vegas.

Cami takes a deep breath and rips the contract in half.

I shuffle back, as if she pushed me.

Jesus, she's done with me too. She just ripped up our marriage license. Like it was nothing but a sheet of paper. Like it doesn't matter.

Like we don't matter.

My gut twists and my hands clench. I pull in a breath, feeling my body begin to shut down as my mind tries to catch up.

Cami doesn't want to wait for divorce papers.

She's done.

I said I was done.

We're just...over.

TWENTY-FIVE

Cami

He's horrified. I note the shock in his expression, the pain in his expression, the desperation that clouds his vision.

The sound of our marriage certificate ripping fills the air. It hangs in the silence that follows, an echo with massive repercussions.

"Leif," I say, my voice eerily calm. Because this is it. This is my gesture. This is me. I'm going to lay it all out for Leif Bang and pray like hell that he chooses me back. "Look at me."

He does, his hands fisted at his sides.

"Our marriage was born out of impulse and reaction. But I don't want to start my future with you on a whim in Vegas. You mean too much to me. You mean everything to me, and I want to do it right. I want to commit myself to you properly. I want our family and friends to bear witness to the love I feel for you, Leif. Because it's big and complicated and messy.

Like me. But no one has ever made me feel whole. Or at peace. Or at home, like you have. I ran because I didn't feel worthy. You're...you."

He shakes his head as if he doesn't believe me. Or can't believe what I'm saying.

"You're larger than life," I explain. "Laid-back and care-free. But committed and driven. You're a star athlete and an amazing person. A model son, a loyal sibling. You're a valu-able teammate and a worthy opponent. You're...you. And I didn't feel like I could ever be enough for a man like you. Not with my past and my hang-ups. Not with my lack of direction and faltering self-esteem. This weekend, I overheard your friends talking about how you don't fail. How you'd never give in and accept defeat. And I knew this because you told me as much. I started to worry that you were only staying in this marriage because accepting that we made a mistake was a failure. A sacrifice. And hell, I hated that. I don't want you to ever settle for less. And I felt less, Leif. No"—I hold up a hand as he opens his mouth to interject—"I didn't feel less because of you; I felt less because I allowed myself to feel that way. And it was time for me to woman up," I toss out Rhett's advice.

Leif shuffles another step closer.

"Running into Levi was by chance. But talking to him made me come to terms with some things that I've held on to for a long time. He had emailed me twice in the past month."

"Seriously?" Leif asks.

I nod. "I'm sorry I didn't tell you. I don't know why I didn't. I just wanted to put the past to rest. And the other day, I did."

"Levi didn't try to...you know?" He gestures his hand in a circle.

"No. Not at all. In fact, he said I deserve a man like you. And that he deserved the hit you delivered."

Leif snorts. "Great. So now I can't even hate him."

I roll my lips together to keep from smiling. "There's nothing to hate because it doesn't matter anymore. He doesn't matter. Your friends' opinions don't matter. The woman from the wedding that you dated—"

"It was a coffee and a lunch," he growls, his eyes blazing.

Oh. Well, that makes me feel better.

But, focusing on the matter at hand... "That doesn't matter either. The only thing that matters is me and you. And the future we claim together. I want to be with you, Leif. Not because of a fun night in Vegas but because I can't imagine a future without you in it. I love you so much it terrifies me. And it's the best type of fear. It's because I care, and for the first time, I truly have something to lose. You. I never want to lose you, Leif, but I understand if my actions make it impossible for—"

This time, he does cut me off. Because he strides to me so quickly, I can't react. Then, his hands are holding my waist, and his mouth is on mine, kissing me hard. "I could never *not* want you, Camille. I will choose you over and over and over again if that's what you need."

"I just need you, Leif. Not a piece of paper. Not a ring, even though I love the purple crown. I don't need anything but you."

Leif chuckles. "I've been going out of my freaking mind."

"Me too. And I'm sorry."

"Don't ghost me, babe. I know this is new and we're figuring things out, but I need you to talk to me. To be honest. To be in this *with* me."

I nod, lacing my fingers with his. "I'm right here. I'm not going anywhere, Leif. Not this time."

"Promise?"

"I swear it." I make an X over my heart, and he smirks.

Then, he drops to his knees. He looks up at me and those electric eyes pin me in place. He reaches into his pocket and pulls out a blue ribbon. A diamond on the end catches the light and I gasp. "Leif," I say slowly.

"I know you don't need the diamond. But I want you to have one anyway," he says sheepishly. Leif looks up at me and for a second, he looks boyish. Vulnerable and thoughtful and more beautiful than any man I've ever known. "You gave me more than stakes, Cami. You gave me everything I dreamed of and with you, I've grown into the man I always hoped to become. Camille Coleman, my heart, will you marry me again?"

I can't stop the smile that crosses my face. "Yes. Always yes."

Leif slides the ring on my finger but keeps his hold on the ribbon. He tugs gently and I drop to my knees, throwing my arms around his neck to kiss him.

Our kiss is edged in giddy delirium. Like a dream come true. We're laughing and crying, a tumultuous coming together of emotions. I let myself feel them all, knowing that this is living. This is choice. This is the euphoria I want.

"I'll never get enough of calling you my wife," he murmurs, kissing the underside of my jaw. "This season, I can't wait to see you wear my jersey. My name and number on your back."

"It'll be my name too," I remind him.

He pulls back and lifts an eyebrow. "I thought you didn't want to be a Bang?"

I shake my head. "I was naïve about that. I want to be a Bang more than anything in the world."

Leif's flingers flex on my hip. "You already are, beautiful."

I keep my arms dangling over his shoulders as I kiss him again. This time it's soft and deep and slow. "Leif," I murmur.

"Yeah?" He buries his face in my neck.

"How long have you been carrying around that ring?" I wonder.

"Over a week. I was going to propose in Honey Harbor," he admits.

I wince, realizing I ruined his proposal. But, if you ask me, this one was better. It was spontaneous and a little bit desperate. Just like us.

"You should probably call my dad," I point out.

Leif chuckles. It's quiet at first but as it picks up momentum, his shoulders shake, and it turns into a full-out belly laugh.

"What?" I ask.

He shakes his head and resettles me on his lap. "Oh, Knox. I already have. Your family's been waiting for you to tell them we're engaged for days now. Well, jury's still out on Cheryl. I think your dad was nervous she'd spill the beans."

My mouth drops open. "Seriously?" Now, I understand Rhett's warning in a different way.

"Seriously."

"I'm so sorry, Leif." I laugh with him. "I made a mess of things. We did... I mean, we did everything out of order." I hold up my hand with the beautiful, elegant diamond shining. I inhale sharply as I admire it. "This ring is stunning."

"You're stunning," Leif says. "And we did everything right, Cami. Right for us and our story. That's what matters."

"That's all that matters," I confirm, kissing him again.

Then, Leif lays me out and we make love on the kitchen

floor in the middle of the day. It's not hurried or frantic. It's not sweet or gentle.

It's pure bliss. Exhilarating and centering and promising.

It's the start of a new chapter in our love story. A story that's perfect for us.

TWENTY-SIX

Leif

"It's good to meet you, Ben," I say, shaking Cami's dad's hand.

"Good to have you here, Leif," he replies, giving me a firm shake.

Cami's sister Jenna pulls me into a hug, Rhett gives me a solid slap on the back, and Cheryl beams.

Today, I meet the family. Tomorrow, we head to Crosslake. And in two days, I marry the woman of my dreams.

Cami slips her hand in mine and draws me deeper into her childhood home. It's wild that she grew up only a handful of streets over from my house. Our paths could have crossed an infinite number of times, yet we met on a random night in Vegas.

If that's not fate, I don't know what is.

"Are your brothers and Annie in town?" Cheryl asks as I take a seat at the dining table. It's already set with a beautiful spread to welcome Cami and me home to Minnesota.

"They're all arriving today," I say, grinning. "Mom's over the moon."

"I bet!" Jenna says, sitting across from me. "Mom hates when Cami, Rhett, and I are away at the same time."

"And that was such a short window," Rhett admits. "Jenna and I live nearby, and Cami stayed local for college."

"Yeah," Ben says, sitting at the head of the table. "Now it's time for Cami to spread her wings." He tosses his youngest daughter a wink.

"Can't believe you're getting married first," Jenna says.

"I can't believe you're getting married at all," Rhett jokes, smiling at Cami. He turns his gaze to me. His eyes are filled with amusement, and I know that he's happy for his sister. While he wasn't thrilled about our Vegas wedding, it was born out of concern for his sister's happiness. I can appreciate that because I'd feel the same way about Annie. "You sure about this, Leif? There's still time to make a run for it!"

Cheryl laughs and pours wine in our glasses.

I squeeze Cami's hand under the table. "More than positive," I say.

Cheryl takes her seat and Ben lifts his glass. "To Cami and Leif. We're happy for you, proud of you, and here for you. Congratulations."

"Welcome to the family, Leif," Jenna tacks on.

"Thank you." I dip my head in thanks and take a sip of my wine. Rhett picks up a serving platter and adds some turkey to his plate. We all dig into lunch and spend a leisurely afternoon around the Coleman's table, talking, laughing, and enjoying time together.

I never thought I'd belong to another family, but the Colemans are pretty special. And, with their proximity to the Bang household, Cami and I continue our family time. In early evening, we head over to see my parents and siblings.

"They're here!" Annie hollers, rushing me. I pull my sister into a hug. "Missed you!"

"Missed you, too," I say. We have a quick thumb war and I let her beat me before I exchange greetings with my brothers and parents.

"It's good to finally meet you," I say, kissing Rory's cheek hello. "Hey, at Empress Hollywood." I hug Jensen's girl, Bailey, and use her gaming handle. "And you must be Gardenia," I greet Jake's woman, who has Ryder on her back, his little arms wound around her neck.

"It's great to meet you, Leif," Gardenia says, a twinkle in her eyes. "And your wife, Cami."

Cami smiles and holds out her arms. I have no idea how, but Ryder jumps into them, forgoing any awkwardness and claiming her as his aunt.

Mom is in her glory, with all her children under one roof. As we settle in the living room, puzzle pieces strewn on the floor and Ryder challenging Tanner to a game of Uno, Dad approaches.

"Dad," I say.

He holds my gaze for a long beat, before smiling. Then his arms dart out and he pulls me into a hug, clasping my shoulder. "I'm proud of you, son. Real proud."

And it hits me unexpectedly. Because yeah, my dad's been proud of my hockey accomplishments for years. But I think this is the first time I've proved to him that I'm grown-up. A man. A man with a wife I plan to honor the same way he's honored Mom.

"I had a good role model," I tell him.

He pulls back, his eyes flaring with unexpected emotion. I chuckle and tap his shoulder.

He turns toward Cami. "I've always wanted another daughter," he admits, surprising everyone in the room.

Cami grins, unflappable and easygoing. "I should warn you, Mr. Bang, I'm a bit of a wild card."

Surprise flickers across Dad's face and then his eyes crinkle. He laughs, louder and longer than I've heard in a long, long time. Then, he pulls Cami into a hug. "Call me Lars, Cami. And I always bet on the wild cards."

My family drifts back to their games and side conversations. There's an absurd amount of appetizers and snack foods. Plus, endless drinks. Naturally, Mom made my favorite banana bread. We order an obnoxious number of pizzas and Gardenia sneaks the twins a few sips of pop.

There's raucous laughter, settling of old debates now that there's more women to weigh in on who was right and who was the asshole, and so much reminiscing.

Cami fits right in. She slides into my life like a puzzle piece, snapping in and making the picture complete. I look around at the faces of my family members and wonder how I got this lucky.

A few months ago, I wondered if I would ever find this. The stability, the love, the trust. And now, I wonder how I lived so long without it.

"To the Bangs." Tanner lifts a bottle of beer in a toast. He glances at each of us Bang brothers and sends Annie a grin. Then he turns his attention to the new women in our world. "And to the women who chose these brothers." He winks at Rory, and she laughs. Then, he gives a full-on body roll, flexing to show off his muscles. "You could have had this!"

"Oh my God!" Cami laughs, smacking a hand over her mouth.

We dissolve in laughter and Jake tosses popcorn at Tanner's head. "You're a goofball."

"Dad! You have to pick up the popcorn," Ryder schools his father.

Gardenia nods in agreement. "And vacuum."

Annie shakes her head and glances at Cami. "You sure you want to marry into this chaos?"

Cami exchanges a look with me, her smile big, her eyes bright. "More than positive."

I lean toward Annie. "You joke now but watch out. You're next in line and while wedding planning may have occupied Mom's time for a few months, I doubt you're off the hook."

Annie's eyes widen.

I snort. "Be on the lookout, little sister. Mama Bang is coming for you next!"

Jensen and Bailey snicker. King nods in agreement.

I sit back and wrap an arm around my girl. We spend time hanging with my family. After Rowan wins a game of Uno, I lean into her side. "Want me to show you my old room?"

King hears me and snorts, giving me a look.

Cami bites her bottom lip and nods. I take her hand and pull her from the living room to the cheers, whistles, and obnoxious comments of my family members.

"Don't do anything I wouldn't do!" Tanner hollers.

"So, anything is up for grabs?" Jake asks.

"Your bed squeaks," Annie warns.

"I shared a room with you!" Jensen reminds him.

Cami dissolves in laughter as I ignore my siblings and pull her into my bedroom. I close the door and she leans against it, crossing her arms over her chest. Her eyes dance when they meet mine.

Amused, excited, happy. She looks at me like she did at the club that night in Vegas. Like our future is filled with possibilities and we're on the precipice of diving in.

"We can't have sex in your childhood bedroom with your family downstairs," she says.

I snort and shake my head. Then, I place a hand on the bedroom door next to her head, dip down, and kiss her hard. "I want to show you something."

She quirks an eyebrow, curious.

I walk to my bedside table and pull out an old journal. I kept it for years. "When I was ten, I wrote down all the things I hoped to accomplish in my life. I would have forgotten all about it, but Mom mentioned writing letters to her friend Diane, who passed recently, and it jogged my memory." I flip to the page and pass it to Cami.

She takes it and bites her bottom lip.

"When I grow up, I want to be a hockey player. I want to learn to surf and travel all over the world. I want to get a big tattoo as long as Mom doesn't get mad. And I want to marry a pretty girl who likes to laugh. She must also like hockey, tattoos, and surfing." Cami closes the journal and looks up, her expression radiant.

"So, I have an important question for you, Camille."

"Shoot," she says.

"Do you like surfing?"

She laughs and it's like music. "I'd like to learn."

I grin and pull her close for another kiss. "Then you're the perfect woman for me. I dreamed you up when I was ten."

She giggles and wraps her arms around my shoulders. "You were pretty smart for a ten-year-old."

"Yeah," I murmur, brushing the tip of my nose against hers. "I knew laughing was important."

She laughs again and my smile widens. Then, I kiss her sweetly.

"In two days, we get married," I whisper.

"And I become a Bang."

"You ready for life with me, Knox?"

"I can't wait, Ten."

"Good," I murmur, kissing her again.

Ryder and Rowan burst into the room and the bedroom door slams off the wall. Cami and I break apart in surprise.

The twins crack up and Ryder holds out a hand. "I knew they'd be kissing."

Rowan grumbles and slaps a five-dollar bill in his waiting hand.

"You two are smart cookies," Cami says, wrapping an arm around each of their shoulders. "Who wants to play me in Uno?"

"Me!" they both shout. Then, they each take one of her hands and pull her back downstairs.

A cheer goes up when she enters the living room.

I stand at the top of the stairs and listen to the conversations, to the excitement, to the love flowing from my parents' living room.

Mom appears at the bottom of the stairs and gives me a knowing look.

"Happiness looks good on you, Leif."

I take the stairs slowly and when I reach the bottom, wrap an arm around Mom.

"Scheming looks good on you," I say.

She laughs.

I kiss the top of her head. "But if you tell any of my siblings I said that, I'll deny it to the death."

Mom wraps an arm around my waist and pinches my side. "I wouldn't expect anything less."

We stand like that for a long moment.

In two days, I'm getting married.

EPILOGUE

Cami

"He's not supposed to see you before the wedding!" Mom says for the third time.

"Mom, it's called a first look," Jenna explains, also for the third time. "It's a thing now."

"It's super popular, Mrs. Coleman," Izzy tacks on.

Mia and Tamara nod seriously while Annie presses her lips together to keep from laughing.

"Just because it's a thing doesn't mean she has to do it," Mom argues.

"Mom," I say, glancing at her in the reflection of the mirror.

She meets my eyes and hers fill with tears. "You look beautiful, Camille."

"Ooh! I said I wasn't going to cry!" Izzy fans her hand in front of her eyes and turns away from the mirror.

I hold out a hand and Mom takes it. I squeeze. "Thank

you. But I want to see Leif. Nothing about us is traditional so why break our winning streak now?"

Jenna laughs.

"Fair point," Annie says.

Mom dabs at her eyes. "Fine. If you insist on having bad luck, go see him before you make me cry and mess up my make-up." Mom reaches for a tissue, which Izzy readily provides.

A knock sounds on the door. "There's a guy here waiting to see you," Rhett calls through the door.

My sister bites her bottom lip and lifts her eyebrows. "I'll go check!" She moves to the door, giving me one final moment.

"I'll follow her because Rhett is hot," Mia whispers.

Tamara rolls her eyes. "She's harbored this crush for far too long."

This time, Annie does laugh. "I hear that. Having older brothers is a curse." She tilts her head and grins at me. "And at times like these, a blessing."

I smile back. Then, I take a deep breath and stare at my reflection. My dress is perfect. The seamstress executed my design perfectly and I revel in the fact that I'm wearing a custom-made design by moi. Leif thinks I should pursue fashion design on the side, since it's something I love so much. It's a path I'd like to consider in the future but right now, I enjoy working with Maria, Tarek, and Sam too much to let those social connections ease.

Besides, I want to settle more firmly into my life, my new beginning, in Knoxville. And I don't want to miss any of Leif's games or opportunities to wear his jersey.

I sway from side to side, my hands clutching at the delicate lace of my gown. My purple ring is on my right ring finger, my diamond engagement ring on my left. "Happy wedding day," I tell myself. Then, I turn away from the mirror and walk to the door. I'm ready to surprise the groom.

I pull open the door to the cottage my parents rented for the wedding, and step into the hallway. "Where is he?" I ask Jenna.

She points toward a room down the hallway that serves as a library. "He's waiting for you there."

I grin and walk into the library.

Leif is standing by the window with his back to me. He's surrounded by sunbeams and books and it's a moment I'll remember for the rest of my life.

"You ready?" he asks.

"I'm ready."

He turns and I revel in the emotions that cross his face. Joy, disbelief, happiness, love.

He blinks back tears, which causes my own emotions to rise to the surface. I blink rapidly.

"Don't make me cry, Ten."

Leif clears his throat and shakes his head, coming toward me. "You're so beautiful, Knox." He takes my hand, cups my cheek, and gazes into my eyes. "I love you so much."

"I love you too." I place a hand on his hip and lean forward to kiss him.

When he pulls back, he keeps my hand in his. "Give me a spin, let me appreciate all your hard work."

I do as he says and love that he studies the details of my dress. "It's stunning," he murmurs. "You're stunning."

"I'm yours," I remind him.

He chuckles. "I know. I can't wait to officially make you Mrs. Bang."

"I'll never hear the end of jokes, will I?"

"Nope! And if we have kids, oh, get ready," he warns me, lacing our fingers together.

"I'm ready for anything if we're doing it together," I tell him seriously.

"Me too, Cami." He brushes his thumb over my knuckles. "Let's go get married."

"Let's get married!" I agree.

And we do.

Surrounded by the love and support of our family and friends, I marry Leif Bang at midday in front of a glistening lake in our home state of Minnesota.

It's a beautiful wedding, a perfect day, and a series of moments I'll never forget.

And at the end of it, the man of my dreams takes me to bed and makes me his forever.

Well, Diane, I did it!

I saw Leif properly married to the perfect woman for him, Cami Coleman. Well, now she's Cami Bang.

Do you remember the Colemans? Oh, they're a wonderful family and they've embraced Leif the same way we've embraced Cami.

Fully, wholeheartedly, and happily.

You would have loved Leif and Cami's ceremony! It was a beautiful and picturesque wedding. Do you remember that summer trip we took to Crosslake? It was a bit like a homecoming—all the kids there together with Lars and me. Plus, Cami spent her childhood summers there.

While these events are certainly joyous occasions, they're also bittersweet since I know your presence would

*have made the day richer. You were missed beyond
measure, but I felt you there in spirit.*

And I needed that, my friend.

*It's hard to believe Kingston, Jakob, Jensen, and Leif
are settled in beautiful relationships. They're thriving,
Diane, and I am truly thrilled. A weight has been lifted
off my shoulders and now, when I slip my hand into
Lars's at night, I know we've done right by the kids.*

*Only Annie and Tanner are left. And you know how
much I adore New York City...*

Until my next adventure!

Love, Stella

THANK you so much for reading Cami and Leif's story! I hope you loved it! Want more Bang Brothers? Make sure you check out LIGHT 'EM UP! **She hates me, but when I'm around her, my skate blade's not the only thing made of steel...**

CLICK HERE TO READ LIGHT 'EM UP NOW>

IF YOU WANT to meet the Thunderbolts—and fall in love with their found family—from the beginning, don't miss Mila and Devon's steamy, workplace romance in *Hot Shot's Mistake*! Intrigued by Levi Rousell? Gain more insight into his backstory in *The Burnt Clovers Trilogy*.

BANG BROTHERS HOCKEY SERIES

Meet the Bang Brothers—five hot hockey-playing brothers who are allergic to commitment.
The brothers are about to face off against their newly-retired mother...who suddenly has plenty of time to play matchmaker. Add in their baby sister and some secret dating, a single dad, an accidental pregnancy, a marriage of convenience, and a wrong bed—or two—and these siblings are not going to know what hit them!

Lace 'em Up
Show 'em How
Hit 'em Hard
Lock 'em Down
Light 'em Up
Hook 'em Hard

ALSO BY GINA AZZI

Tennessee Thunderbolts:

Hot Shot's Mistake

Brawler's Weakness

Rookie's Regret

Playboy's Reward

Hero's Risk

Bad Boy's Downfall

Lock 'em Down

Knoxville Coyotes Football:

Faked and Fumbled

Surprised and Sacked

Trapped and Tackled

The Burnt Clovers Trilogy:

Rebellious Rockstar

Resentful Rockstar

Restless Rockstar

Boston Hawks Hockey:

The Sweet Talker

The Risk Taker

The Faker

The Rule Maker

The Defender

The Heart Chaser

The Trailblazer

The Hustler

The Score Keeper

Second Chance Chicago Series:

Broken Lies

Twisted Truths

Saving My Soul

Healing My Heart

The Kane Brothers Series:

Rescuing Broken (Jax's Story)

Recovering Beauty (Carter's Story)

Reclaiming Brave (Denver's Story)

My Christmas Wish

(A Kane Family Christmas

+ *One Last Chance* FREE prequel)

Finding Love in Scotland Series:

My Christmas Wish

(A Kane Family Christmas

+ *One Last Chance* FREE prequel)

One Last Chance (Daisy and Finn)

This Time Around (Aaron and Everly)

One Great Love

The College Pact Series:

The Last First Game (Lila's Story)

Kiss Me Goodnight in Rome (Mia's Story)

All the While (Maura's Story)

Me + You (Emma's Story)

Standalone

Corner of Ocean and Bay

ABOUT THE AUTHOR

Gina Azzi writes Contemporary and Sports Romance with relatable, genuine characters experiencing real life, love, friendships, and challenges. Dive into her sports romance series: Knoxville Coyotes Football, Boston Hawks Hockey, and Tennessee Thunderbolts or get lost in her rockstar romances in The Burnt Clovers trilogy.

A Jersey girl at heart, Gina has spent her twenties traveling the world, living and working abroad, before settling down in Ontario, Canada with her cover model husband and three littles. She's a voracious reader, daydreamer, and coffee enthusiast who loves meeting new people.

Connect with her on social media or through www.ginaazzi.com.

ACKNOWLEDGMENTS

I am thrilled to be back in the Tennessee Thunderbolts world with Cami and Leif's story! I had the best time diving into their complicated—yet amusing—marriage of convenience.

It's an honor to collaborate with Elise Faber, Jami Davenport, Kat Mizera, Kelly Jamieson, and Cathryn Fox. What an amazing time we had creating the Bang Brothers—don't forget Annie—and their wonderful hockey royalty family! I can't thank them enough for such a wonderful experience!

To Amy Parsons, Erica Russikoff, Virginia Carey, and Amber — thank you for your time, insight, and love for this story! A big thank you to Ann Jones and her team at Milk & Cookies! A shoutout to Jena Brignola for designing such awesome covers.

And thank YOU! To every reader, blogger, bookstagrammer, and romance reading enthusiast who took a chance on my words, who supported this series, who backed this Kickstarter, and who picked up Leif and Cami's romance—thank you from the bottom of my heart. Your support means the world to me!

To my home team—my husband Tony and our littles A, R, + L—I love you all the world!

Made in the USA
Coppell, TX
28 August 2024

36562368R00152